THE RAGS OF TIME

Escaping an emotionally unbearable life with her husband, Hannah flees with her young daughter to the town of Malpas, where she hopes to uncover her family's past and build a new life. Arriving with no wedding ring and baby Vinnie tucked under her shawl, Hannah struggles to find a place to stay. As nightfall approaches, she stumbles across a cottage owned by kindly Widow Nightingale, who takes them in — but will Hannah be able to find work, build a stable life for her daughter, and discover happiness in the town?

PAMELA KAVANAGH

THE RAGS OF TIME

Complete and Unabridged

LINFORD
Leicester

First published in Great Britain in 2011

First Linford Edition
published 2019

A catalogue record for this book is available
from the British Library.

ISBN 978–1–4448–4291–3

For Mary Perry,
in appreciation of all the years
of friendship, encouragement,
and a shared love of books.

1

'Sorry,' the landlady said. 'The room is not available.' The door of the lodging house was shut in Hannah's face and as if in protest, the child in her arms began to grizzle.

'Hush, my lamb. We'll find somewhere, never fear.'

A thin October wind flurried, tugging at Hannah's bonnet strings and sending a swirl of leaves rustling around her feet. Crooning to the baby, she drew her shawl closer around the two of them before picking up her bulging carpet bag and heading blindly off along the street in her quest for bed and board.

Hannah had not expected this. She had been so pleased to arrive here, excited even, and being turned away yet again from what had seemed a suitable place to stay had come as a shock.

Around her, the little market town with its backdrop of the rolling hills of Wales bustled with activity. Women with laden shopping baskets and small children in tow threw curious glances at the arresting young stranger with the babe who had arrived in their midst.

Tradesmen and merchants going about their daily business sent Hannah the odd nod of greeting, one being so bold as to doff a cap. Hannah walked on, her heart quailing a little. Her mother had always painted such a glowing picture of Malpas. What if she could not find anywhere to live, now that she and her daughter had come here?

She threw a glance over her shoulder, fighting down a fear that she was being followed by someone. All along she had done her best to avoid detection, sneaking out of the house in the small hours before the maid who saw to the fires was up and about; mindful to avoid the main highways, keeping to the more unfrequented raikes and lanes where there was less chance of discovery, her direction guided by the flow of the river and the passage of the sun.

It had been three days now, three long days of dread at being spotted and taken back in disgrace to the man she called her husband, of snatching a few hours' respite in an isolated barn or derelict cottage before scuttling on with her child clasped in her arms, bent on putting as much distance between them and home as possible. So far her attempts at subterfuge had paid off — but Edward had contacts. A man on a fast horse could soon catch up with a lone traveller and her precious burden.

On the third morning the rumble and clop of a horse-drawn vehicle had alerted her to fellow travellers and she had darted behind a tree to hide — too late, for she had already been seen. They had pulled up, a band of swarthy-faced copers in a painted wagon, southward-bound to a horse fair. They had offered a lift for the final leg of the journey and been kind to her, sharing their meat and fire and finally dropping her off on a grassy heath outside the town.

'You travel a lonely road. May luck go with you, rawnie,' the Romany wife had said.

Having reached her destination, Hannah had thought the worst of her worries over. Negotiating a problem in finding a room to rent had never entered her head. It would have to be temporary measures for now, she decided, just until she found something more permanent.

She waylaid a passer-by on the street. 'Excuse me. I am new in town and seeking accommodation. Please could you recommend a hotel?'

The man looked at her covertly. Hannah suspected that her travel-worn appearance was less than encouraging and was not surprised when his blunt country face filled with doubt. 'Well, The Crown has a good name, mistress, though I'm told they charge a pretty penny. You might be better with The

Red Lion. Carry on up the street and it's on the left. 'Tis a rough and ready sort of place, mind.'

'The Red Lion?' Hannah found a smile. 'Thank you, sir.'

She soon came to the inn. Low-roofed and timber-framed, its wattle cracking was shabby and a rowdy group of revellers were blocking the doorway. It was not exactly what Hannah had in mind, although smoke streaming from the chimneys spoke enticingly of warmth and comfort within.

'Sir,' she called to a man who was rolling kegs of ale into a shaft beneath the building. 'I am looking for somewhere to stay and I was directed here. Can you help?'

Again she felt herself subjected to close scrutiny as the innkeeper took in her crumpled clothes that, though plain, were obviously of quality. His gaze came to rest on her face, a perfect oval set with long-lashed dark eyes and a mouth that was made for laughter.

'Have you no maidservant with you,

mistress?' the older man enquired.

'No. I am travelling alone,' Hannah replied.

'I'm sorry, ma'am, we don't take lone females here. Why not try the New Inn at Hampton? It's a coaching stop on the Chester Road and you might be luckier there. 'Tis a fair tramp, mind.'

He pointed the way and Hannah set off, retracing her steps out of the town. She felt vulnerable, since this looked to be a major highway and every rider and carriage that passed felt a threat. The baby and her luggage were heavy, and the mile and a half felt more like ten. She breathed a sigh of relief when the inn came into view.

Here, she again made her request and her heart fell when the man shook his head.

'Sorry, ma'am. We've just had a party of travellers in off the Stage and every single room is taken. The wife's rushed off her feet. Have you asked in the town? There's many a housewife there offering lodgings.'

'I have come from there. They were either full up or . . . ' Hannah shrugged, and hitching the infant onto her other shoulder, she tried again. 'Please, sir — couldn't you find us a room, if only for the night? I should not mind sharing. It will soon be dark and my child needs shelter.'

'I'm sorry, lady. It's more than my life's worth to take on another guest. They're even sleeping on the taproom floor. Scuttling round like a scalded cat my good woman is, what with the extra cooking and whatever.'

From inside came the sound of laughter, a voice shouting for more ale, the pert reply from a serving girl.

'Albert? Albert? Are you going to be out there all night? I need a hand in the kitchen,' hollered a female voice from the corner of the building.

Throwing Hannah a regretful glance, for it went against the grain to turn away a pretty face, the innkeeper departed.

Hannah watched him go, crushingly

aware that there was nothing for it but to try again in the town. She snatched a few moments to find a quiet spot to feed the child, choosing the sheltered seclusion of a stand of oaks that were holding on to their leaves in defiance of the season. Then she was walking again, keeping to the shadow of the high hedges and pulling out of sight whenever a traveller approached.

Back in the township of Malpas she made her enquiries and was directed further along the street, to a row of humbler cottages that opened straight onto the road.

'Alone, are you?' The woman at the first port of call folded her arms across her ample chest, her gaze going pointedly to Hannah's ring finger and the telltale lack of a wedding band. 'This is a respectable establishment,' she said, face tightening. 'I only take gentlefolk here. You might try Ellie Porter at number seven. She's less particular.'

It turned out that number seven was

full up. 'I'd heard a young woman with a babe was looking for lodgings. On your own, are you, dearie?'

'Yes,' Hannah answered defiantly, ruffled by the knowing look and suggestive words.

'Hoity-toity, aren't we? There's some as need to mind their p's and q's when they're talking to decent folks.'

'I'm sorry,' Hannah was quick to say. 'Do I take it you have a room, mistress?'

'No, I haven't. You'll be fortunate to get anywhere in the town at this hour, and you a woman alone. I'd try your luck further out. Happen a good wife at a farmstead will take pity on you.'

'Thank you,' Hannah said, turning away with tears in her eyes. In the streets a suggestion of righteous disapproval was now on the air. Storekeepers were finishing for the day, shutting up shop and pulling down blinds. One, a candle-maker, sent Hannah a smile but in the main she felt herself uncomfortably in question as she trudged on, pulling uphill towards a looming square-towered church, her little daughter growing heavier with every step.

Vinnie was awake again and beginning to cry quietly. Maybe they'd take them in at the rectory for tonight, Hannah thought with a fresh leap of hope. Tomorrow she could try for something more permanent. Things always looked better in the light of a new day.

She was passing the churchyard when it momentarily crossed her mind to wonder how many of her forebears rested there. Once she was safely settled here, she would go and look. There could even be living relatives in the town, some of whom may remember her mother. There was no possibility that she could disclose her background, but it would be heartening to know that someone of her own blood resided here.

At the rectory gates Hannah hesitated, her heart failing her. She had not missed the eyes sliding in silent question to her wedding finger, before gliding over her travel-stained clothes and mud-encrusted boots. Looking at her face crowned with burnished dark hair, the expressions of the women offering bed and board had said all. *Young miss with an infant? This one was no better than she ought to be!*

Well, she could not help her looks, nor could she reveal that she had traded Edward's nuptial ring with a pedlar for cash in hand. No one must know why she was here, she told herself. No one must learn her secret.

Abandoning the idea of respite at the rectory, Hannah continued on her way. None of the timbered and thatched dwellings she passed displayed a bed and board notice in the window and her dismay increased. Daylight was fast thickening to dusk. She had to find somewhere soon.

Presently she was leaving the township behind, passing a milestone marked Cuddington, the carved black lettering standing out starkly against the white-painted stone. The place name was not familiar and with nothing but open fields and woodland on either side, the landscape becoming featureless in the gathering dusk and rising mist, Hannah began to feel truly lost. It seemed as if she had been on the road for weeks rather than days, supplementing the cheese and bread she had brought with her with roadside berries and sour little apples plucked from the hedgerow.

You travel a lonely road. May luck go with you, rawnie.

The Romany wife's words rose in her thoughts and a wry smile touched her lips. At this moment her road looked very lonely indeed. *Help me*, she prayed. *Don't let me have to spend the night under a hedge like a common vagrant.*

As if the fates were listening, Hannah spotted a light ahead. Unwittingly she had turned on to an unmade country lane, off which stood a small white-walled cottage. From a range of outbuildings at the back could be heard the mournful lowing of cows and the sleepy clucking of roosting fowl.

Small, neatly hedged fields held rows of what looked like vegetable crops; onions and cabbage, turnip and parsnip. A trap pony grazed in an orchard and it glanced up at her curiously, before dropping its head again to get on with the serious business of eating.

Taking a hopeful breath, Hannah trudged up the garden path and rapped on the cottage door.

It was opened by a short, spare woman, not young, lamp in hand. Her greying brown hair was tucked into a widow's cap and Hannah thought she must have been newly in from tending the animals, for she wore an oversized drabbet smock over her gown of modest homespun. She held the lamp higher, the better to see her caller.

'Yes?'

'Please, ma'am, have you a barn where my child and I might spend the night? I can pay,' Hannah added hastily.

The woman hesitated, and giving them a searching look, her face softened. 'A barn's no place for a mother and babe, methinks. You'll have tried the town?'

'Oh, yes. The inns are either full up or . . . well, there did not seem to be any board to be had at Malpas. It was suggested I tried the outskirts and now it's getting dark and I must find a place soon.' Sheer weariness was making her gabble and she stopped abruptly and rocked the child, whose mewling was becoming a wail.

Her mind made up, the woman stepped aside. 'You both look fit to drop. Come along in, daughter. A speck by the fire is better than a draughty barn.'

Grateful beyond words, Hannah stepped into the small houseplace which displayed an almost fierce cleanliness and much evidence of make-do-and-mend. A pot bubbling on the hearth gave off a mouthwatering smell and Hannah's stomach growled in response. The breakfast of dry bread and strong tea was aeons away and not a morsel of food had passed her lips since. She had expected to dine tonight at some comfortable lodgings and be abed by now, justly nervous of what the future might bring but satisfied that so far her goal had been reached. How mistaken could one be!

The woman pulled up a stool to the fire. 'Sit you down. Make yourself at home. Here, give me your shawl and bonnet. That's right. What a sweet babe. Would the dear soul be a boy or girl?'

'A little girl.'

'There then, and growing as pretty as her mammy. How old is she?'

'Not twelve months yet.' Hannah sank down on the seat and gently rocked the wailing bundle. 'I call her Vinnie and I'm Hannah. Hannah . . . Morgan,' she said, pouncing on the first surname that entered her head. Real names were traceable and Hannah did not want that. She was finished with Parkgate and her husband's everlasting tantrums and resentment. As to her given name — well, hers was commonplace enough to pass unnoticed and Vinnie was her special one for Virginia, so Hannah saw no problem there. Then again, she would have to be cautious and choose her words with care in the future. Any small indiscretion could spell disaster for them.

'Morgan?' The woman frowned in thought. "'Tis Welsh, I'm thinking. You are not from these parts, then?'

'No ma'am, I'm not.'

'I see. Well then, Hannah Morgan, I'm happy to make your acquaintance. I'm Widow Nightingale — Madge Nightingale, though no one has called me that for many a year, not since my man passed on.' She smiled, a little wistfully. 'But there, you've come far by the look of it. You must be famished. There's a rabbit stew on the hob. 'Tis poor fare but you're welcome to share it.'

Over the meal washed down with small ale, Hannah touched once more upon the raw subject of how unfortunate she had been in her search for lodgings.

'I've been looking since noon. None of the inns would take a woman alone. Neither would any of the townspeople offering bed and board. I was beginning to think I'd never find anywhere.'

'I'd heard how there was a young woman with a babe seeking a room. The post-boy mentioned it when he called. You mustn't take it to heart. Newcomers always arouse suspicion no matter what the place.'

'I'm quite respectable,' Hannah said, flushing indignantly. 'I'm not what they think.'

'Be patient. Folks will come round in the fullness of time.'

Faintly through the ill-fitting casement drifted the sound of a fiddle and a male voice, singing a song of lost love and the yielding promise of spring. Hannah glanced up.

'It's only the gypsies,' Widow Nightingale said. 'They gather on Overton Common every year on their way south.'

'I travelled part-way with them. They seemed a kindly people. At least, so I found. I have always been rather fearful of them in the past but I can see now that I need not have been. They could not have been more helpful.'

'I've never found them a problem, though there are some that wouldn't agree. There's many a fowl goes missing or a cow robbed of her milk come morning when the gypsies are around. Folk make doubly sure to lock up their animals at these times. Come to think of it, happen the people in the town took you for one of them, you being so dark and turning up at the same time. 'Twould have added to their caution.'

'What? A gypsy? Me?' Hannah made a choking sound in her throat. 'Never!'

'Ah well, people are quick to jump to conclusions. Now then, let's get you both settled . . . '

A short while later, lying on a makeshift pallet in the corner of the room with Vinnie fed and changed and snug beside her, tired though she was Hannah could not sleep.

Her husband's face rose in her thoughts; furrowed, jowly, reddened in rage. How had he reacted, she wondered, dread striking her, when he had found them gone, deserted by his wife and child, albeit the child being a daughter he had not wanted?

A girl? Another wench? What use is that to me! Fie, madam, you try me sorely! Where is the son you promised me? Where?

Spat in anger, the words hammered still on Hannah's mind. In vain she had protested, telling him they had to be thankful that the child was vigorous; that she was young and would bear more children; and there was every chance of the next being the son he wanted.

Edward would have none of it and she could still recall his angry words.

Excuses! Women's talk! Do you think I've not heard all this before? It was all the first Mrs Pennington ever said — God rest her soul. I'm not one to speak ill of the dead but enough's enough. What have I done to be so accursed? Me, a devout member of the Church, never been known to miss a Sunday, give generously and willingly to the coffers, no matter how bottom-less they appear, pray on my knees for God to grant me this one small request. Why is it that the lowliest farm worker can sire a brood of lads and all I get is prattling females that need marrying off? Dowries to find! Did you think of that, madam, when you presented me with yet another?

It had been so unfair, so deeply hurtful, and in her weakened state of childbed the tears had been swift to flow.

Edward, having no time for snivelling women, had made his retreat, stamping from the bedchamber and its mealy smell of birth and echoed pain.

Biting her lip, Hannah made a huge effort and turned her thoughts to brighter issues — and the generous presence of the woman who had taken them in.

Widow Nightingale had asked no questions, though something in her direct nut-brown gaze suggested she suspected a mystery here.

Hannah liked the way she'd been called daughter. It made her feel less alone in the world. The woman had been kind to Vinnie too, providing water in which to wash her and cuddling her in her arms while Hannah prepared for bed.

In due course Hannah's lids grew heavy and she slept. Her slumber, however, was tossed by dreams; strange, disjointed.

2

A bright fire burns in the grate and there is a fresh smell of beeswax and soft soap.

The cobbler's wife, trim and youthful-looking, presides over the laden tea-tray in her best gown and frilled apron, lace fichu at her delicate throat. Opposite her, the caller stirs her tea in a rose-patterned china cup. She is a thin-faced woman, stiffly laced into an old-fashioned gown of black silk. A small girl plays at her feet.

'Come, child. Sit here and drink your milk like a good girl,' the woman says.

Pouting, the child obediently takes the cup she is handed and sips, shuddering. The cobbler's wife gives a small exclamation of concern.

'There then, my pretty. Don't you like my good fresh milk? It's from

Emmeline, our best cow. Emmeline will cry if you don't drink it up.'

'I never can get her to take her milk.' The other woman sounds anxious.

'Happen it's a tad rich for her. Here, child, let me pour you some goat's milk instead. Have some of my seed cake to help it down. It will bring the roses to your cheeks.'

She goes to the table under the window and exchanges the milk, cutting a small slice of cake into dainty pieces before bringing the fare back to the hearth.

Once the child is happily settled, she turns back to her guest and offers more tea.

'I am glad to see you. You must call any time. You mustn't feel you have first to ask. Anything we can do to help — '

'Thank you; that is most kind. I am sure we shall become used to everything, given time.'

★   ★   ★

Hannah woke with a start to the shrill cry of a cockerel and the clatter of milk pails. 'What a strange dream,' she murmured, frowning. It had been so real. She might almost have reached out and touched the child.

She searched her mind for the little girl's name, if indeed either woman had called her by it. It seemed imperative that she should know it, but already the dream was fading as dreams do and Hannah dismissed the matter as the result of an overtired body and overstretched mind. At her side Vinnie began a hungry mewling that effectively drove the last traces of the dream away.

'There then, my sweet. What a good sleep you've had.'

As Hannah fed the baby she collected her thoughts. She had managed it! She had left her marital home and all it represented and come to the small township in Cheshire's rolling farm-lands that had meant so much to her mother. She remembered her vow to discover where her mother had lived and find out if any relatives remained — but discreetly, dropping one question here, another there.

The outside door opened to admit the woman who had taken them in. A thick, woollen shawl was pinned crossways over her chest and she carried a jug of frothing new milk and a willow basket of eggs.

'Ah, so you're awake! Good morning, daughter.'

'Good morning, ma'am,' Hannah answered, suddenly shy.

'A fine one it is, too. You were both sleeping so soundly I didn't want to disturb you. No doubt you'll want to wash. Pump's out in the yard. There's a bowl and soap in the wash-house.'

Hannah struggled to her feet in her creased petticoat and chemise, trying to push back her tumbling cloud of hair with one hand whilst holding the baby in her other arm.

Putting the milk and eggs on a shelf, Widow Nightingale turned to her. 'Here, give the child to me while you get dressed. I've brushed the mud from your gown but I fear it still bears the marks of travelling.'

'That was good of you. I have something else to put on. I must look for permanent lodgings today. Work, too. I need to make myself presentable for that.'

Hannah reached into her carpet-bag for the single change of undergarments and plain woollen skirt and high-necked cotton blouse she had brought with her. Other than a pelisse and bonnet, all the other items of luggage were Vinnie's. Who would have thought so small a person would need so much? After three days on the road, the greater part of her daughter's wardrobe required washing, too. Deciding to leave these problems until later, Hannah handed the infant into the older lady's outstretched arms and went to find her way to the pump.

Shortly afterwards, the dust and sweat of travelling washed away and clad in fresh clothes, her hair tied temporarily back with ribbon, she felt more herself.

She was astonishingly hungry and made short work of the bowl of porridge the widow provided, sitting back in her chair to sip a cup of hot, sweet tea — made from a third straining by the look of it, but thirst-quenching nonetheless.

'I've been thinking,' Widow Nightingale said, dandling the baby on her lap. 'After my Judd passed on I had a notion to take a lodger. The extra pennies would have come in handy but I kept holding back and the weeks became months — and, well, a body gets used to her own company. You turning up like this, out of the night and needy . . . some would say it was meant. You're a quiet-spoken young woman and the babe is no trouble. If you're agreeable, you can bide here with me at Brook Cottage.'

'Oh!' Relief washed over Hannah in huge waves. 'Ma'am, I'm so grateful.'

'I confess the rental will come in

useful. I've lived hand to mouth since my Judd went. If you could lend a hand about the place as well, that's all to the good.'

'You have work for me?' It seemed too good to be true. 'I know how to milk a cow and see to the animals. I can cook and clean. And I — '

A wave of a hand silenced her. 'Daughter, you see for yourself how things are here. What I scratch from my few acres just about makes me a living. It was different when my man was alive. Judd was a cobbler and we lacked for little then. Taken before his time, he was, but there it is. No, what I meant was I'd appreciate a hand with the extra washing and preparing of meals and such like. You'll have to look elsewhere for paid work, I'm afraid.'

'Oh.' Hannah bit her lip. 'Yes, of course. Of course I'll pull my weight and assist you as best I can.'

'I knew I could count on you. Now, about the rent.'

She named a sum that was not

excessive. Hannah mentally calculated that she had enough from the sale of her wedding ring and her mother's gold pin to keep them for a few weeks. The locket containing a curl of her mother's hair hung still on a narrow ribbon at her neck, hidden under her chemise where she had placed it before leaving the house. The pieces of jewellery that Edward had given her she had left behind. She'd not add theft to her other sins and besides, she wanted nothing of his.

'You can have the back bedroom. It's small and south-facing so it gets the sun. It can be hot in summer, but nice in the winter with the sun at the window. There's a crib you can use for the babe. It was intended for our little ones, but 'twas not to be.' Widow Nightingale shook her head sadly, shrugging. 'Come, best I show you.'

The room held a narrow iron-framed bed with bolster and patchwork cover-let, a tall chest of drawers and single wooden chair. Sprigged curtains, their rosebuds long faded, fluttered at the window and there was a rag rug on the planked floor. Hooks for outdoor clothes decked the latched door. Above the bed a worked sampler proclaiming grace and virtue to be one's guide provided a splash of colour. A small washstand holding a large floral bowl and matching jug completed the furnishings.

Looking round, Hannah's spirits lifted. 'Widow Nightingale, this is perfect.'

'It's no palace,' she replied. 'But it's clean and that's the main thing.'

'Before we continue I must make something clear. My child was not born out of wedlock. Yesterday when I was looking for lodgings, well, it seemed to me that people had the wrong impression of me.'

'Yes, you as good as said as much last night.'

'I wanted to clarify it. They were wrong about me. I was not expecting it and perhaps that was naïve of me.

Anyway, that's said and I feel better for clearing the air. I'll just add that for reasons best known to myself I cannot say why I am here. I cannot thank you enough for trusting me and taking us in. We won't be any bother to you, I promise.'

'Bless you, daughter, I never doubted it for one moment. And you have every right to your privacy. This is a quiet community here at Cuddington. We're away from the town and the prattle. It does have its advantages.' She made a rueful quirk of her lips. 'Well then, since we are to share a roof, you'd best call me Madge. I'd like that.'

'And I'm Hannah.'

They exchanged a smile. The first approaches of friendship had been made.

'The crib's in the attic. You'd best help me fetch it down and we can give it a polish. This way, Hannah. Mind the stairs. They're narrow.'

* * *

31

It did not take Hannah long to put away their belongings and make up the crib with warm blankets. The day was blowy and she washed the simple dove-grey gown and petticoat she had travelled in and Vinnie's little frocks and clouts, pegging them out on the line in the orchard to dry. It had been more than three years since Hannah had done work of this kind and in that time her hands had become soft and white.

Not for much longer, she thought as she chopped wood for the fire and peeled vegetables for the pot, bent on making herself useful while her landlady was occupied with the animals.

As well as a couple of milch cows, there was a small herd of goats, a flock of poultry and the trap pony that Madge laughingly said had a trick of making himself scarce when he was required.

'Quiet as a lamb he is once he's caught. Do you know how to manage a pony and trap?'

'Yes, I do. I can do most things around a farm. I thought to try for dairying work or cheese-making. It must be a place where I can keep Vinnie with me. Could you recommend anywhere?'

Madge considered, head to one side. 'There's Overton Hall. It's a popular workplace and they seem to do pretty well for staffing, so they may not have any vacancies. The little one may be a handicap, too.'

'Do you think so?' Hannah was dismayed. 'They never minded babies and small children going with their mothers at . . . where I've come from. So long as the work was done was all that mattered.'

'You'll find it different here. There's no shortage of workers in the town. Employers can afford to pick and choose.' Madge broke off, smiling. 'Don't worry about the babe. She's a bonny little maid, bless her. Happen we can come to some arrangement over her.'

Hannah's heart stabbed. Being parted from her child would be a wrench and she clutched Vinnie to her, fierce in her love for the baby. Yet reason told her she may not have any choice in the matter. She had to earn a living and Madge's words made perfect sense. Yet still she hesitated.

'I know it's hard but you might find it in your best interest, daughter,' Madge said quietly.

The gentle term of address was Hannah's undoing. She gave a nod. 'Well, all right. I'm sure she'll be in good hands, won't you, my lamb?' The baby cooed in response and both women smiled. 'I'll take her with me today. You never know, I may be lucky and the sunshine will do Vinnie good. Overton Hall, you say? Is it far from here?'

'Mile or so if you take the Old Lane. It's quicker across the fields. I can point you in the right direction, though don't get your hopes up. Whether they'll have a place is anybody's guess. Had you thought of a cleaning job or shop work?' Madge pursed her lips doubtfully. 'Failing that, there's always the salt mine.'

'Salt mine?'

'At Lower Dirtwich. It's no short walk, mind, especially in the winter when the roads are bad. Hard graft, too. The mine is where folks go when there's no other work to be had. Prosser will always take people on.'

'Well, it's worth keeping in mind. I'll try the farms first. They should have something, even if it is only potato picking while the season lasts.'

'That's back-breaking labour for a woman. Indoor work is more suited to a genteel young thing like you. I know I painted a gloomy picture of the town but you might give Malpas a try; see if there is anything to be had there.' She gave a smile of encouragement. 'I'd better get on. Best of luck, daughter.'

Hannah had the feeling she was going to need it.

At around mid-morning, she coiled

up her hair, put on her pelisse and matching bonnet and with Vinnie set off along the Old Lane — no more than a cart track, deeply rutted from the constant traffic of farm vehicles and horses' hooves.

Overton Hall was an imposing building of gabled roofs and weathered black and white timbering. A late rambler rose was in bloom over the porticoed entrance, its blush-pink petals throwing out a heady scent.

Hannah continued round the corner of the house to the rear, her boots crunching on the gravelled pathway. Here were yards, outbuildings and bustle.

She approached a dairymaid, a plump girl with a snub nose and straggling straw-coloured hair bundled up into a cap. Her smock was soiled from toiling in the milking-shed and across her shoulders was a yoke bearing two brimming pails of milk.

'Please, miss, I'm looking for some work. Could you tell me where to ask?'

'You're the third this week. It's Stan Palmer you want to see. He's the boss here. I shouldn't be too hopeful. The others got turned away. Well, they're choosy who they take on here.'

'It's worth a try,' Hannah responded. She liked the look of the property and the girl had not been unfriendly. Her fingers were crossed as she moved on. She found the head man in a cheese room, checking the vats for mould.

'Yes?' he asked curtly.

'Please, sir. I'm looking for work.'

His shrewd gaze took in her mode of dress and her face, bringing back yesterday's experience in all its grim detail. Vinnie gurgled at him, holding out a chubby hand.

'Dairying's a skill, mistress,' the man said, ignoring the baby who frowned and sucked her fist.

'Oh, I know that, sir. I can do it; butter-making, cheese, everything. I can milk as well. I was milkmaid on a farm when I was a young girl.'

'Is that so?' He looked dubious. His

gaze went to the child in her arms. 'What of the infant, mistress? You'd have to leave it at home. We can't have babes in arms here. It's against the rules, you understand.'

'That's all in hand. I've made arrangements for my child.' Hannah looked at him with hope. 'You've something for me?'

'I didn't say that. Would you be the young woman who was looking here, there and everywhere for lodgings yesterday?'

'I . . . yes,' Hannah admitted.

'Thought as much. Caused quite a stir, didn't you? It isn't every day that happens.'

'Really?' Hannah couldn't help but say. 'Malpas is only just off the main highway to the city of Chester. There must be many a lone traveller wanting a night's respite.'

'Not women with no maidservant or nursemaid accompanying them. Sorry, lady. We've no work here. Good-day to you now.'

Mortified at the inference once again that her respectability was questionable, Hannah left the premises with as much dignity as she could muster.

It was the same at a farm called Alport and others she approached. One, Middle Farm, offered to take her name in the event of a vacancy but stressed that it was not likely to happen until the spring of next year.

Hannah had now been out for a while and she stopped by a stile to rest, dropping Vinnie a kiss on her chubby cheek. She wondered how she could bear leaving her child in the care of someone she scarcely knew . . . but the need to find a position was uppermost. Before the day was out she must get a place.

The sun was still high and Hannah decided to do as her landlady suggested and try the town. It was a long trudge across the heath. She skirted the common where the gypsies had camped. They must have left at dawn, for the only signs of habitation were the circlets of grey ashes from doused fires and the deep tracks of many hooves and wheels on the soft ground.

She came to a fork and took the turning for Malpas. Hedges on either side were bright with crimson berries of holly and scarlet swags of rowan.

Hannah wondered if her mother had come this way as a girl, picking cowslips by the brook, fishing for minnows in the shallows. Her mother had been a Carraway before she had married Hannah's father. It should not be difficult to trace the name, she thought.

She came to the mill, its wheel whirling busily. On the cobbled forecourt a man was loading sacks of flour onto a cart, the horse standing patiently between the shafts. He was a giant of a fellow with springing red hair and an enormous red beard, and he sang as he worked; a country song of pretty maids and first love, much the same as the gypsy's of last night.

Hannah found the miller's burly frame more than a little fearsome, and tightening her grip on her child she quickened her step. However, the man had already seen her.

'Good morrow, lady,' he called out. 'Grand day, isn't it?'

'Yes, it is,' Hannah called back hesitantly.

'Just what we need for putting us on for the winter. What's called an Indian summer and long may it last. I like the autumn, myself.' His voice was cheering and Vinnie laughed and waved and the miller sent the infant a grin and waved back.

Hannah was aware of him watching her as she walked on. The song started up again.

Fair maid, where are you going?
Why look you so sad . . . ?

The fine baritone voice became part of the swirl of the mill wheel and the calling of larks high above. The sun shone brightly, that beguiling October sun. Hannah thought of her fisherman father whom she had adored, lost at sea in an autumn storm when she was just a child. She thought of her mother and how she had slaved long hours in the fields or on the quayside, taking any work to be had and earning a pittance to keep a roof over their heads. That sort of life had not been for her, Hannah had silently decreed when her mother had been unable to carry on, weakened by a lung condition that left her coughing and gasping for breath.

Within the month her mother was dead, worn out before her time, and Hannah was alone. It was her good fortune that her mother had been an educated person and made sure that her daughter benefited from her learning. Hannah, thinking to better herself, had taken a chance and advertised her services as a governess — and so Edward Pennington had come along.

It had only been a matter of time before he was swearing that he loved her and would wed no other. A widower in his late fifties with a brood of girls from a first marriage, Edward had a large house, servants, and horses in the stables. *What woman wouldn't have been tempted*, Hannah thought with the bitter benefit of hindsight.

Marriage to the elderly, respected member of the community who spent long hours at the boatyard where his fortune had been made was not what Hannah had expected.

The house that had seemed so grand had turned out a prison. She was expected to grace Edward's table and his bed and nothing more. Recalling the wet kisses and unloving embraces, she shuddered.

The housekeeper, a harridan of a woman who ruled the staff with a steely thumb, had seen to it that her new mistress's influence on the house was negligible. Hannah hadn't even been allowed to choose her own maid, much less organise the meals or keep her own household records. Stifled, she had taken to showing an interest in the administration side of her husband's business. Edward had shown a grudging admiration for her abilities and

43

quickness of mind. He had even allowed her to record the accounts when his man-of-work had been temporarily indisposed by illness.

Then Vinnie had been born.

'A girl! Another wench! What use is that to me? Fie, madam, you try me sorely!' he had shouted.

Once her strength and vigour had returned after the ordeal of childbirth, Hannah had sought her husband out and pleaded afresh that next time it could be the son he wanted to inherit the Pennington fortune. Edward would have none of it. His stubborn denials and corrosive bitterness had destroyed the last vestige of feeling she felt for the man who had purported to have plucked her from the gutter and made her his wife. His accusations were not strictly correct, though there was no arguing with Edward and Hannah had turned sadly away.

Then there had been the overseer at the boatyard, a beefy fellow with an eye for the ladies and an inability to keep his hands to himself. Hannah shuddered again, cursing the day she had been born a beauty and not unremarkable like other girls.

Lost in thought, she came into the town and stood a moment to get her bearings. Malpas itself consisted of a main street on a hill, crossed by another at the top — Church Street and Well Street respectively. Mouthwatering smells of new bread drifted from a bakery shop across the road from the school, and on impulse Hannah went in and spent a precious penny on a small loaf. She sent the woman a smile.

'Please, ma'am, I am looking for work. Have you any in the bakehouse?' she asked.

The woman, stout and cheerful, looked her up and down. 'From these parts, are you?'

'No ma'am, though I have come to live here.'

The woman was not to be put off. 'From Chester, then?'

'No, ma'am, I'm not a Chester person.'

'Happen you'll be from the Wirral. I had an aunt who lived on the Wirral and she spoke like you. Would that be Willaston or maybe Heswell?'

This was getting too close to the mark for comfort. Hannah gave her head a shake. 'Ma'am, you are mistaken. I'm a simple country woman and no one could call me anything else.'

'Ah well, so be it. You'll be Widow Nightingale's new lodger, I don't doubt.' She chuckled, pleased at having guessed correctly. 'News travels fast here. Is there no husband about?'

The baker's wife's directness was disconcerting and Hannah started to stutter and stumble. 'N . . . no, ma'am. That is . . . I mean to say — '

'Widowed then,' the woman put in. 'I am sorry. You're young to be so blighted, and with a child in arms too. Still, you're a good-looking young woman. No doubt you'll find someone else before long.'

Hannah felt the guilty heat flooding her face. 'Ma'am, please have you any work? I'm good at reckoning. I could serve in the shop, anything.'

'No, no, mistress. Me and my man are more than able to manage the place between us. Try the Cuddington baker. 'Twould be more convenient for you than here.'

Thanking her, Hannah left the premises. In the street she broke off a corner of the loaf for Vinnie to gnaw on and put the rest into the deep pocket of her skirt before striding on, her head high, aware of the interest she aroused in the gossiping groups of women on cottage steps and in shop doorways.

She forced herself to offer a murmured greeting, and was heartened when it was returned by one or two women. The majority, however, merely stared and some turned deliberately away, as if the ground was contaminated by the comely young woman with no wedding band and a child displayed so blatantly in her arms.

Suddenly wearied of it all, she made a slight detour and slipped into the churchyard to study the inscriptions on the gravestones for signs of her predecessors. To her disappointment the first few rows revealed none bearing the name Carraway. Disheartened, Hannah gave up and resumed her search for work.

On Church Street she tried the apothecary's, the draper's, candle-maker's and the milliners opposite. Saddlers, boot and shoe maker, clock maker, maltster. Every one had the same answer — *sorry, no*. It brought home to Hannah that Madge's assumption that the town was well supplied with workers was not wrong, and it fell to reason that a local person would be taken on before a stranger; and one with a question mark over her head at that.

Not to be daunted she continued her mission, calling at another baker's premises on the road out of town. Again she was unsuccessful.

Neither, more depressingly, was the Cuddington baker able to oblige. Hannah arrived back at Brook Cottage tired, aching and more than a little despondent.

'Any luck?' Madge enquired, accepting the loaf of bread she was handed.

Hannah shook her head. 'None whatsoever. No one needed an extra hand. Unless 'tis me they don't want.'

'Take heart. Finding work isn't easy, I did warn you. Did you try the farms?'

'Every one. This isn't the best time of year for work on the land, is it? They're turning people off, not taking them on.' Hannah shrugged. 'I went by the mill. There was a man loading a cart. Would he be the miller?'

'Big fellow? Red hair, eyes like sapphires? That'd be Cameron; Miller Blake's eldest. Do anything for anyone, will Cameron. He's betrothed to Lizzie Marsh from Alport Farm. There are two more Blake boys. Thomas — he's the good-looking one, wants to go to sea but his da has other ideas. Then there's young Will.' Madge shook her head wordlessly. 'Such a rip of a lad! Always into mischief as a little'n' and he doesn't change much. He's got in with the wrong crowd if you ask me. Never knew his mother. She died when he was in the cradle. Happen that's his problem.' As she was speaking Madge was mashing tea in the brown pot. She gave the faded leaves a determined stir. 'Shame you didn't find a place, Hannah.'

'I shall keep looking. Maybe tomorrow I'll strike lucky.'

★　★　★

For the rest of the week Hannah scoured every corner of the town and outlying hamlets, enquiring at dwelling houses, trading yards and shop premises for a vacancy. The answer was always the same. *Sorry, no.*

One good thing was a slight lessening of the suspicion and animosity Hannah had first experienced. It looked as if the

50

town was coming to accept the stranger with the pretty child who had appeared so mysteriously in their midst.

There were some, however, who still treated her with misgiving, as if they felt there was more to her than met the eye, and it was this that made Hannah doubt that she would ever find employment here.

'What will you do now?' Madge said. 'Go back to where you came from?'

'No, not that! I'm here — and this is where I'm staying.'

'Then it looks as if it will have to be the salt mines. Heaven help you, daughter. Picking potatoes in a muddy field is a pleasurable occupation compared with that.'

Hannah's heart fluttered in fear, though it wasn't the nature of the work that was her worst dread. She knew how people in business tended to communicate no matter what the nature of the trade, and with a mine being a going concern with a stringent system of recording all who worked there, right down to the lad who ran the messages, there was a chance of her whereabouts being revealed. Admittedly it was a very slender chance but there all the same, and the knowledge filled her with foreboding. Inwardly berating herself for not having had the foresight to take on an entirely different identity and shrug off her given name along with her married one, Hannah met Madge's steely gaze with dull resignation.

'So be it,' she said, and had to wonder all over again what the future held for a woman in her position, with little money, a failing self-esteem and a guilty secret that was already threatening to weigh her down.

3

Right from the start she hated it; hated the rough talk of her workmates, the dirt and squalor, and the sting of raw salt on tender flesh. With her sleeves rolled up and a square of coarse cotton protecting her hair, she joined the team of women at the mine face to stack the heavy blocks of salt or sift the residue into tall barrels. In Prosser's mine, she was to learn, not a grain was wasted or someone paid for it.

'Weston Prosser is said to be something of a rough diamond. I'd watch myself if I were you,' Madge had warned her.

With the words of caution ringing in her ears, Hannah had been mindful to keep her eyes lowered as she stood before the owner of the mine in the dark little office with its smell of ink and dust and a window that looked out over the mine workings.

'Work, is it?' Weston Prosser, a blunt-faced fellow in gaiters and frock coat, ran a hand over his beard in thought. 'You'll be the young widow that's set all the tongues wagging, I warrant.'

Far from easy at the deception, for she was all too aware of how a mild untruth had a way of growing, Hannah felt she had no alternative now but to go along with it.

'Yes sir. I am she.'

'There's a child, is there not?' Prosser continued.

'Yes sir.'

'Hmph! Name?'

'She's called . . . my daughter, do you mean?'

'Your own name, woman,' Prosser said in a growl that would have made the staunchest heart quail.

Hannah's cheeks flushed. 'Oh! I'm sorry. It's Hannah, sir. Hannah Morgan.'

'Right then, Hannah Morgan. We'll see how you make out, shall we?'

'You'll take me on?'

'For now. You'll have to pull your weight, mind. There's no room for shirkers in my mine.'

'Sir, you misjudge me!'

Far from being annoyed at the rebuke, a flicker of amusement crossed the not unhandsome face. 'Well, well, like I said, we shall see about that. Here then, mistress. Put your mark there.'

Prosser shunted an open ledger across the table, pointing to a line on a page. Hannah took the quill he offered and unthinkingly wrote her full name in a neat hand, ending with a little flourish.

The mine-owner sat back in his chair, regarding her narrowly through shrewd hazel-green eyes. 'So we have a scriber in our midst. That's rare, that is. That's very rare indeed. Tell me, Hannah Morgan, when can you start?'

'As soon as possible, sir,' Hannah said.

'Women don't go down the mine shaft, you understand. They generally work on the surface. The girls will show you the ropes. The men work in shifts but the womenfolk work a ten-hour day, starting at seven. You get fifteen minutes' break at noon to eat your snap. Mind you bring food with you; we can't have workers flaking out for want of victuals. Wages stand at one and tenpence a week, money docked off your account if you're late.'

Hannah bit her lip. It wasn't much but it would cover the cost of her board and Vinnie's fostering, and leave a penny or two over to add to her savings.

Under the grimy window a lady assistant sat writing, her quill scratch-scratching in the silence, a frown on her narrow face. She was perhaps in her early thirties and had sandy-coloured hair screwed back in a tight, unforgiving bun. Slightly protruding light blue eyes travelled with disdain over Hannah's youthful form and face.

'That's it, then,' her new boss said abruptly. 'And seven sharp, remember.'

'Very well, sir,' Hannah said.

She had not liked the way his gaze had followed her as she left the premises, but at the very least she had work and for that she was thankful.

★　★　★

Lower Dirtwich itself was no more than a straggle of cottages set among rolling hills, with the odd timber-framed farmstead set back off the road. The three-mile walk in the dark hour before dawn promised to be lonesome and from the first Hannah made sure to acquaint herself with her workmates, some of whom came from the Malpas region and agreed to her walking along with them.

'You'll be the young widow-woman,' said Maisie Gregson. She had a permanently dirty face and was missing a front tooth, but her smile was warm as she strode alongside Hannah in her ragged homespun, wooden pattens on her feet. 'Someone said there was a child.'

'Yes, a baby girl. Vinnie. I've . . . I've had to leave her with my landlady,' she said looking down.

'That must have been hard. Still, Widow Nightingale's a good soul and you'll see your babe when you get back. Just think, if you'd gone into service you'd only have got to see her on your afternoon off; once a month if you were lucky.'

'Yes, there is that. I've had to wean her quickly. Madge is feeding her goats' milk and pobs. I hope she takes to it all right.'

'She will. Our mam swears there's nothing better than goats' milk for a babe. Mam brings them into the world, so she knows these things.'

'Your mother is a midwife?'

'You could call it that. She does the birthing and the laying out,' she explained.

'Oh, I see.' Hannah fell into silence as they tramped along in the foggy pre-dawn cold.

'Cheer up. Things could be lots

worse,' Maisie rejoined.

It was Maisie who showed her how to wield the sieve and keep up a steady rhythm so that the salt ran swiftly into the barrel, and how to lift the rough-hewn blocks of salt without putting too much strain on the back. Softened from long months of genteel living, Hannah's whole body ached at first but gradually, muscles honed from a girlhood of labouring in the fields reasserted themselves.

The work was strenuous, the hours lengthy, and at the end of the day she arrived back at her lodgings filthy and almost too exhausted to eat the bowl of broth Madge pushed into her hands. Breasts that throbbed with unshed milk within their tight bindings only served to add to her discomfort. It was far, far worse than anything she had done before but she persevered; heartened that she was able to pay her way.

'That Lower Dirtwich is an out-of-the-way sort of place. I don't like to think of you tramping all that distance in the bad weather to come, let alone working all day in the snow and rain,' Madge said as she sat one evening at her spinning wheel, bobbin rattling busily. It was Saturday and Hannah had dragged in the tin bath that hung on a nail outside the back door, filled it with water heated over the fire and with a block of coarse yellow soap. had scrubbed away the sweat and filth of the week. Clean and fresh, this was the longed-for moment when she began to feel normal again. She leaned closer to the crackling flames to dry her long hair.

'It's work. It's all I could get,' she said to Madge,

'All the same, it's not right.' December was here and a cold wind moaned in the chimney. 'It's to be hoped we don't get the snow just yet. It came early last year, Roads blocked, ice on the pond, drifts everywhere. The market at Hampton was closed for weeks; nobody could get there. What a time we had of it.'

'Did you? How strange. It wasn't too bad on the coast.'

The words slipped out before Hannah knew it and she bit her lip. As a rule she was mindful at not giving away anything relating to her past life and in general she succeeded, but tonight, relaxed and warm in front of the fire, her guard had slipped. To her relief Madge carried on spinning as if she had not heard.

'We don't usually get it till January. Days lengthen, cold strengthens, my mother used to say. There's a lot to these old sayings. Don't know what happened last year, I'm sure.' Madge collected another fistful of creamy fibre from the willow basket at her feet. 'Oh, while I think on it, I've come across a piece of flannel in the coffer. It'll make some warm petticoats for our Vinnie.' She paused in her work, reached into a sewing basket on a low table at her elbow and withdrew a length of quality fabric, which she tossed across to Hannah. 'See what a nice feel it's got;

just the thing to keep the little mite toasty warm during winter, methinks.'

'Madge, you mustn't. You may need it for yourself,' Hannah began, but Madge was adamant.

'Fie, it's but a scrap I must have picked up from the pedlar at some point. Have it and welcome. You know by now that Madge Nightingale doesn't take no for an answer!'

Madge's goodness manifested itself in many ways and Hannah blessed the day she had arrived at the widow-woman's door. All the same, no matter how much she counted her blessings, nothing could take away her sense of loneliness and isolation. At Parkgate where she had been born and bred, she had belonged. Constricted and dismal her married life may have been, but as wife to a noted name in the community she had had a degree of standing. There had been people she knew and who knew her. Here, she had no one. She was an outsider with none to call her own. It crossed her mind to wonder if anyone had thought to put flowers on her mother's mound in the corner of the bleak little coastal churchyard. Delyth, Edward's youngest daughter whom Hannah had cautiously befriended, may have done so, though given the current situation — she being a wife reneging on her marriage vows — perhaps not. Hannah knew herself to be a pariah in the eyes of society and would wake in the night, racked with guilt at what she had done.

Stepping out into the punishing dark and cold of a winter morning, her mind had inevitably sometimes flown to the day she had awoken between silken sheets to the sound of the maid refreshing the bedchamber fire. Sipping her morning chocolate, she had listened out for the step of the nursery maid bringing her tiny daughter to her, after she had sent away the wet nurse and insisted on taking the responsibility for her baby's nourishment upon herself.

It had been the one time in that

suffocating, domineering atmosphere that she had truly asserted her authority and Edward, bent on shrugging off all contact with his child, had brusquely told her to do as she pleased. Recollection of his scowling face and snarled words was all it took to make her lift her chin and step squarely into the murk to join her fellow workers, most of whom were in awe of the newcomer in their midst and tended to keep their distance. Maisie alone remained loyal and Hannah was glad of her company during those first tortuous weeks at Prosser's mine.

'Still here, then?' The amusement in her employer's eye as he counted out Hannah's weekly wage one ice-bound Saturday did not escape her notice. 'What a surprise. You are something of an enigma, Hannah Morgan. You intrigue me.'

Hannah did not know how to answer and wisely held her tongue. Prosser's curiosity, however, would not let go. Regardless of the waiting queue of workers anxious to get home to their firesides, he leaned his elbows on the scuffed mahogany desk and regarded Hannah closely.

'Not from these parts, are you, lady?'

'No, sir.'

'No sir!' The words were mocking, the tone not unfriendly. 'I confess I like a mystery. Young widow with a child, comely to look upon. Not uneducated, if instinct serves me right?' He broke off. 'Well, madam?'

'Sir, it is true I have the benefit of some schooling.' She had her mother to thank for that. Alice Carraway had been more than adequately schooled by the aunt who had brought her up and Hannah could only guess at the effort it must have been for the overworked and ailing woman to make sure that her daughter was not lacking in that direction. Night after night, in the feeble light of a taper, Alice had instructed her in the art of penning, reading and numbering. From her father Hannah had learnt the various points of the globe and both parents had contributed to making the history of the realm a storytime not to be missed.

Prosser smiled. 'I thought as much! Well, well. It seems to me your talents are wasted on the mine face.'

'It suits me, sir,' Hannah said, making an obvious show of wanting to be gone by pocketing her payment.

She fled the office, uncomfortably aware of the shuffling steps of the people behind her as they moved closer to the desk and the disparaging sniff of office assistant Felicia Black.

Truth was, she lived in fear of Prosser's interest and did her utmost not to attract his attention on his daily inspection of the works. All the same, she was increasingly conscious of his gaze on her, curious, biding his time. Persons of his standing spelled danger, she reminded herself. They wielded power, knew how and when to assert their authority. It would not take much for him to discover her secret and she agonised lest she had not covered her traces sufficiently well.

The festive season brought a welcome day of respite from the din and squalor of the daily round. At Brook Cottage they celebrated with a Christmas fowl and a pudding made in October. There were comfits for Vinnie, bought with a few precious pennies from Hannah's stash, and an orange that made the child's eyes water but had her groping for more of the juicy relish.

Up until now, so exhausted had Hannah been that she had slept deeply, and if she had dreamed at all it had been in snatches, all trace gone on awakening. That night, however, saw a return of the strange dream she had known when she had first arrived here.

★ ★ ★

Midsummer, the trees in heavy leaf. From the lean-to on the side of the cottage where the cobbler is at work issues the sound of hammering. A dappled pony and high-wheeled trap is pulled up beside the gate. Aboard is the woman in black and the child.

'Madge, I was passing and thought I would call. Will I leave the pony and trap here?' The woman alights from the trap before turning to help the child down.

'Yes, yes. Judd will see to it. How good it is to see you. And the child, dear goodness, how she grows! Are you drinking up your milk for your aunt these days, my pretty?'

The little girl gives a nod and then shakes her head, pouting.

'She likes it no better,' the aunt says. 'Lemonade is more to her taste, I fear.'

'I have some inside, fresh made this very morning. Come along in, both of you. I shall mash some tea and you can tell me your news.'

They proceed into the cottage. The woman takes the seat by the fire whilst the cobbler's wife busies herself with kettle and teapot, fetching the best china from the dresser on the wall, setting the tea-tray with a freshly-laundered cloth.

'Have you been to the mill recently?' she enquires, once they are settled with their tea and cake.

'Indeed. We were there just last week. They all worry about the brother.'

'The sea-going fellow? Well, 'tis to be expected.' The cobbler's wife's voice lowers. 'And you, my dear. How are you managing with the little one?'

'Managing? Indeed, 'tis not an issue. I hope I know my duty and besides, she is proving of little trouble to me. Come, child. Mistress Nightingale has lemonade for you.'

'May I see the kittens?' the child lisps.

'May I see the kittens — what?' her aunt reminds her.

'Pwease!'

'Bless the lamb, of course you shall. You shall have one for yourself, providing your aunt is agreeable?'

'Oh, Auntannie! A kitten of my vewy own! May I have it? May I if I say pwease?'

The cobbler's wife throws the other woman a questioning glance and receives a small nod of acquiescence. 'There then, 'twill be a bonny pet for you, a little kitty-cat . . .'

* * *

Hannah woke abruptly, the voices singing in her ears. Who were they, the austere-looking aunt and the child? Where she used to live, there had been a wise-woman who said that in certain circumstances the past would reach out to people in their dreams. Waking dreams, she had called them. She had regarded them with something akin to awe. At the time Hannah had dismissed the talk as the patter to be expected of the rather daunting woman who lived in a shack in the hills and could be seen gathering seaweed on the estuary. Now, however, her heart gave a flutter of alarm.

What did it mean? Was it a warning, a sign to go back to her husband? She could not, would not do it! Lying wakeful in the warm bed, Hannah tossed and fretted till morning.

Overnight the wind had changed direction and it was back to work in the first blizzard of the season, her shawl wound around her head against the deep, penetrating cold. The dream was soon forgotten. Reality was the rough banter of her workmates, the rumble and thud of the mine workings and the bite of salt against chapped, sore flesh. So it continued, day after gruelling day — until one morning in the middle of January when Hannah was summoned to the office.

A leaping fire of coals in the iron grate gave off welcome warmth. Hannah saw that the small desk under the window lacked the usual occupant. Trying to overcome her nerves, she faced her master across the larger desk on the far wall.

'You sent for me, sir?'

'Aye. I seem to recall that you have some education, madam. I know you pen a fair hand. So tell me, does that skill extend to reckoning too?'

'I'll not deny it,' Hannah answered, mystified.

Prosser barked out a sequence of figures and demanded the total, which Hannah supplied. She had always been quick at adding and subtracting.

'You have a sharp mind, lady. But there, you must be wondering what all this is about. Truth is I find myself in a quandary. Miss Black is confined to the house at present. Some mishap on the ice, a sprained ankle, the messenger said. Think you could stand in for her? 'Twill be worth your while, I promise.'

He named a wage that set Hannah's mind reeling. 'Well, madam?' he questioned.

Hannah caught her breath. The offer felt too good to turn down but caution prevailed. 'May I enquire the nature of the work, sir? I have some knowledge of book-keeping, though I cannot confess to being highly experienced.'

Prosser waved her words aside. 'I don't doubt you'll be able to follow Miss Black's figuring. It's just a matter of recording the wages, ditto the in-goings and out-goings, and seeing to the correspondence, of course. None of it beyond your capabilities, I warrant.'

'Sir, one hopes not.'

'You'll do it? I'll not beat about the bush, mistress. You'll be getting me out of a hole if you take this on. I'm a busy man. I have neither the time nor the inclination to interview every might-be-suitable female in the district, when I know for a fact there is a perfectly adequate one in my own mine. Well, what say you?'

Still Hannah hesitated, but only briefly. 'Thank you, sir. I'll be pleased to accept,' she heard herself saying in a voice that seemed to come from far away.

'Good, good. All sorted, then. Present yourself here in the morning at say, eight of the clock? I'm thinking you'll find this manner of work more to your taste, Mistress Morgan.' He went to the fire and stood with his back to it, legs straddled, fingers twirling the side-whiskers he was inordinately proud of. He sent her a smile. 'Till tomorrow, then?'

He went to open the door, letting in a blast of frosty air, the rumble and thud of the mine workings, the shouts of the men and bawdy laughter of the women. It was only as Hannah hastened home to tell Madge of her good fortune that it crossed her mind to wonder what she may have let herself in for. To be closeted day in, day out with Prosser was a situation not to be taken lightly. What if he was another prone to taking advantage of a helpless female, as Madge had once as much inferred?

Other thoughts crowded in. Would she be able to keep her secret? What if her boss know her true identity already and was indulging a game of cat and mouse? He struck her as a man who liked to play games; shrewd, intelligent, not above taking it on himself to delve into her past, should he have a mind to. What if she arrived one morning at her place of work and came face to face with her husband?

Hannah's insides churned at the prospect. Another doubt was the work itself, and all the old familiar dread of tomorrow settled at the pit of her stomach. She couldn't help thinking that life was like hurtling down an icy slope on a sleigh, powerless to stop, and when she reached the bottom, what then?

4

To Hannah's relief her fears were not justified. Prosser treated her with the utmost respect and was ever ready to answer any query she might have concerning the work. He gave every appearance of having accepted out of hand her supposed situation as a young widow and subsequently the dread of discovery receded a little.

A suitable mode of dress had posed a problem. The everyday woollen skirt and blouse worn at the mine-face were decidedly the worse for wear and her only gown she liked to reserve for Sundays. With reluctance she spared a few hard-earned pennies on a length of rust-coloured bombazine and another of calico from the pedlar-man who called each week and spent the greater part of the night stitching her 'office clothes' to wear next day. It was worth

76

the effort to see the look of approval on Madge's smiling face when she appeared, serviceably dressed for her new position.

'That's more like it. I never did care to see you going to join those rough women. You look very nice indeed, daughter.'

'Thank you,' Hannah murmured, her fingers sliding surreptitiously to her neckline to check that her locket was safe. Working on the mine-face she had feared for its safety and hidden it away under her mattress in her room, but now she had taken it out again and it lay flat and solid between her warm skin and her chemise, a poignant reminder of her mother.

Madge sat down to spoon a breakfast of bread soaked in goats' milk and sprinkled with sugar, into the child's mouth. 'What did those others have to say about your new status? Plenty, I don't doubt!'

'Maisie was pleased for me. It won't be permanent, Madge. Once Miss

Black recovers her strength I shall have to go back to the other work.'

'Let's hope it won't be for a while,' Madge said comfortably.

★   ★   ★

Before long Hannah developed a sneaking admiration for Weston Prosser. He worked all hours, dealing with the wages, making new contacts, supervising the staff, and was not above rolling up his shirt sleeves and knuckling down to some hard labour alongside the men when a bout of sickness in Malpas laid many workers low.

Hannah had worried about Vinnie, for there were children who lost their fragile hold on life as the epidemic raged through the town. Cuddington, less than a mile away, kept mercifully free of the infection and as the worst passed Hannah became less worried. She was grateful how her child kept in good health, thanks to Madge's stringent care.

Vinnie was walking now, toddling after the widow as she saw to the animals. Hannah dipped yet again into her savings and bought a necessary pair of sturdy little boots. She was glad of a hand-out of children's clothing from the Rectory, not new but still with plenty of wear in them, that fitted Vinnie perfectly.

For herself she picked up some quality cast-off garments at the market to supplement her office blouse and skirt, and spent the evenings altering them to fit. She had lost weight in recent months and her waist was back to the span it had been as a girl, before the inevitable spread of childbearing had taken its toll.

One dull morning in late February, she glanced up to find her boss looking at her.

'You frown, Hannah. You'll get wrinkles if you're not careful. Do you find the light poor in here?'

'No, sir. I do well enough by the window, though I agree that the office is a little dark. A lamp on your own desk might be no bad thing. Poor light is not good for the eyes.'

'You are concerned for me? Well, well. In all the time Miss Black has worked here she has never once ventured a word of thought on my behalf.' Prosser threw a glance around. 'It's a dismal workplace, I warrant. A coat of whitewash wouldn't come amiss, don't you agree?'

'Sir, I would not presume — '

'Oh, fie, Hannah! I may address you thus? I'd not be so bold as to say it in front of the workers. Miss Black condescends to being called Felicia when we are alone here. Felicia . . . 'Tis a pretty title, if ill-suited.'

'You must call me what you will,' Hannah said, ignoring the rest. She made to return to the letter she was penning but Prosser evidently wanted to talk.

'May I ask who taught you to write so elegant a hand? Did you have the advantage of a governess?'

A picture of the mean little fisherman's cottage where she had grown up rose in Hannah's mind and she almost choked. 'Indeed, no. I thought I had mentioned that my mother taught me all I know.'

'And very thoroughly too, may I say. Are you a reader, Hannah?' he questioned.

There had been a library at Croft House. The columns of leather-bound books that had never before left the shelves, bought for their looks rather than enjoyment, had been her saviour in the past. 'I could be if I had the time,' she said.

Prosser smiled, looking at her intently. 'I have a great fondness for Mr Dickens. Have you read any of his works?'

'Why, yes. The Brontë sisters, too. I have a liking for their poetry,' she confessed.

'Poetry, is it?'

He sounded scoffing and Hannah blushed. To hide her confusion she picked up a wodge of papers, affecting to study them. Prosser chuckled.

'Come, ma'am. I do but tease, though if it's poetry you're after I doubt you'll find it in these parts. Ah, one moment . . . ' He rummaged in the top drawer of his desk and, bringing out a slim volume bound in soft brown pigskin, he brought it across and dropped it in front of her on the desk. 'Do you like Tennyson?'

'You read Tennyson?' Hannah said, surprised. 'Oh, forgive me, sir. I didn't — '

'Nothing to forgive. None would expect it of a rough sort of fellow like me. Salt mining is what's in my blood, Hannah. Started as a boy at the pithead and worked and slaved to better myself and I'm proud of it. I shall never forget the day I was able to buy Lower Dirtwich with cash made from my own sweat.'

Hannah stared at him.

'You think me coarse? A yokel, one not above bragging over my position?'

'No, sir. You are my superior. I have every respect for you.'

'You have a pretty turn of speech. How did you come by it? Was it at your mother's knee, the same as your learning?'

'My mother was gently-spoken, 'tis true. She made sure that I should be so.'

Marriage to Edward had done the rest. To please him Hannah had worked hard to curb her country vowels and master a more gentrified manner of speech — and much good had it done her.

'You're frowning again. You wear your emotions on your sleeve, lady. Would that I could read them.'

She was saved from giving a reply by the works hooter signifying the end of the morning. Beyond the window the women thankfully put down sieve and pail and moved in a gaggle to the shelter of one of the wooden sheds to scoff down the food they had brought with them, before the hooter called them again.

Prosser indicated the Tennyson with a motion of his hand. 'Please take it, Hannah. I have others. I don't want it back.'

'Sir, I cannot.'

'Fiddle! You are an intelligent woman. 'Tis natural to have a thirst for matters way and beyond the adding-up of columns of figures and the penning of letters to folks who fail to pay their bills. Read the Tennyson, Hannah. Let me know what you think.'

'Thank you,' Hannah answered quietly.

Clearly a turning point had been reached. Hannah did not know whether to be glad or sorry.

★ ★ ★

Another two weeks went by and still the assistant did not return. When March arrived, and then April, Hannah began to wonder if her improved position might be permanent after all.

'I made enquiries about Felicia Black

at Hampton,' Madge said, home from market and putting her feet up. 'She's not been seen at St Oswald's for weeks and she's a regular attendant as a rule. Happen she's not able to come back to work. 'Twould do you a good turn, Hannah.'

'It must be hard to be indisposed and not able to see a light at the end of the tunnel. Though I'd be telling a fib if I said I didn't prefer the office to the other, not to mention the better wage it provides.' Her savings were growing, and with them had burgeoned vague thoughts of buying her own property at some point. 'No, I don't dislike the job at all,' she added, holding her hands to the fire, for the spring had come in wet and cold.

'It's just Prosser,' Madge observed, astutely.

'He's not what I thought. He's never anything but polite.'

'Happen folks have got it wrong about him. When you think on it, a bachelor living alone, only a housekeeper and an outside man to see after that great posh house of his on the Wrexham road, people are bound to wonder. All that talk about women and fast living could be nothing. If what you say is right and work is all he's ever done, happen he's had no time to cast around for a wife. This could be your lucky chance, daughter.'

Hannah stiffened. 'Madge, what are you saying?'

'Well, you could do worse than to wed him.'

'I've no wish to marry,' Hannah said sharply. 'I fare very well as I am. There is Vinnie to think of.'

'The child wouldn't be a drawback. Likely Weston Prosser would provide a fine nursery for the little maid. He'd be a father to her, alongside other children you might have. You'd lack for little, mind me?'

'That's as maybe.'

'Hannah, you're young yet. You don't want to be alone for the rest of your life, surely?'

'Madge, please,' Hannah cried. 'If

Weston Prosser has thoughts in that direction he will have to look elsewhere.'

It was boldly spoken but inwardly Hannah quailed. Her employer might be justified in having some interest in her, but if this was the case how would she keep him at arm's length without jeopardising her position at the office? Why, she wondered, did she have to attract men in this way when she did nothing to encourage it?

Perhaps because of the additional unease, the dreams returned. Hannah would hear the voices — the women talking, the child playing, the gruff male tones of the man she assumed to be Madge's late husband, Judd Nightingale, and the tap, tap, tap of a hammer as the cobbler went about his daily work.

She would see the figures taking tea or in conversation at the gate where the pony and trap waited. Once, she caught a fleeting impression of Madge standing in the front, as if watching the lane for a visitor who did not come. All was hopelessly jumbled. She would catch names that vanished on waking.

'Madge, do you ever dream?' she asked as they sat one Sunday eating their breakfast porridge, the child sitting between them. Madge had persuaded Hannah to go with her to the chapel at the end of the lane, a rare event, for her lodger was unaccountably reticent over attending. There was time yet before they needed to leave and Hannah pressed her point. 'Do you?'

Madge chuckled. 'Bless you, daughter, I dream all the time. Everybody does.'

'I don't mean the usual dreams. These are more like scenes going on around me. As if I am there and yet not there — oh, I don't know. I'm not making much sense, am I?' She smiled.

Madge looked at her strangely. 'What are these dreams about, daughter?'

'Brook Cottage mostly, though not as it is today. It is more like how it must have been in your younger days, I would say. Madge, did your husband conduct his work in the little lean-to across the yard? The place at the back of the old wash-house and the wood-store.'

'That's right. Spent all day out there, did my Judd. I use it to store jumble now. Mercy on us, don't say it's my man you're dreaming about?'

She looked so alarmed that Hannah regretted having brought the subject up and hastily tried to rectify it. 'Oh, 'twas nothing. I must have eaten something that disagreed with me. Mr Prosser brought in some seed cake his house-keeper had made. It was heavy and dry, nothing like yours, Madge dear. It must have been that.'

★   ★   ★

'Thank you, Mrs Jackson — an excellent meal as always.' Prosser sent his housekeeper a smile and rose from the table.

'Glad you enjoyed it, sir. Let me put

your coffee on the side table, nice and handy. Can I get you anything else? A nice slice of my rich plum cake?'

The rack of lamb and bread and butter pudding that followed had been filling in the extreme and Prosser resisted. 'No, thank you. I couldn't manage another morsel. Maybe later.'

Once the housekeeper had gone Prosser lit an after-dinner cigar, blew a fragrant cloud of smoke into the air and looked about him. Firelight danced on polished brass and copper and high-lighted his collection of bone china figurines that complemented the solid mahogany furniture and the heavy brocade hangings at the window. He had seen a room such as this as a nib of a lad, peeking in at a window in the town, and had vowed to have one like it one day.

Ambition gained, he thought now, a familiar loneliness sweeping over him. What he needed was a wife sitting opposite, who shared his interests and was pleasing to look upon. An image of

Hannah Morgan presented itself. What an enigma she was! He had seen her once with the child and thought what a picture they made. He drew again on the cigar, wondering why she was so reluctant to talk about her past. It was almost as if she had something to hide. An open book in many respects, she remained tryingly closed in others and he felt fit to wonder if there was more to Hannah Morgan than was obvious.

What was she hiding? It should not be too difficult to find out. Prosser sat back in the chair and drew yet again on the cigar, watching the smoke rise and fade to nothing.

★　★　★

A week later Hannah arrived at Lower Dirtwich to find, to her surprise, that her place in the office was already occupied. Felicia Black looked up from her perusal of the books.

'Oh, Morgan,' she said coldly. 'Mr Prosser had been called away, some urgent business requiring his attention. It falls to me to tell you that you are to return to your previous occupation at the mine-face. Your wage will be adjusted accordingly, taking into consideration that you are — ' she consulted the plain-faced clock above the mantelpiece — 'precisely one hour and five minutes late. The women begin work at seven, as you know.'

'Ma'am, if I had been aware of the change of circumstance I would have adjusted my presence here accordingly,' Hannah said in her own defence.

'That will do, Morgan. Any argument and I shall have to inform Mr Prosser.'

Swallowing the bile that rose to her throat, Hannah turned and, with a fleeting sense of regret for the gown of fine blue kerseymere she was newly wearing, went to join her previous workmates at the mine face.

She was met in the main with sneers and taunts that were not entirely unexpected and the day proved long and hard. Some time during the late afternoon Prosser returned. His face was frowning and the horse was lathered and blowing, as if it had been ridden too hard over too many miles.

A short while afterwards the foreman came looking for her and informed her that she was wanted in the main office.

Prosser, standing in his usual stance with his back to the fire, wore a grim expression. If anything it was worse, and Hannah's heart constricted. 'Mistress Morgan. Madam, I regret to have to say that Miss Black has been going through the books and has found some discrepancy in the figures.'

'Discrepancy?' This was the last thing Hannah expected. She looked in bafflement from one to the other. 'I don't understand, sir.'

'To put it more bluntly it appears that last week's payroll does not add up correctly and in no way tallies with Miss Black's own figures. The rest has yet to be scrutinised, but it appears that a sum of two pounds five shillings has gone astray from the cash box. Where has the money gone, I wonder?'

'Sir!' Hannah gasped. 'You do not think . . . you are not accusing me of theft?'

Prosser's face tightened. 'I'm disappointed, madam. I had thought better of you. In the usual circumstances I would not think twice of calling in the Law. As it is, you had best take a week's wage and go. There will be no references, naturally.'

'Go? But . . . but Mr Prosser, there must be some mistake.'

'No mistake, I assure you.'

'I did not do it!' Hannah said stonily. 'I have done nothing to warrant this. I would never steal. Never! Such a thing would not enter my head.'

Prosser met her words with a cold silence and Hannah stammered to a stop. She looked again from her employer's set face to the calmly indifferent visage of the woman at the desk that Hannah had almost come to regard as her own. The atmosphere told her how useless it was to continue to protest her innocence. Mutely she took the money that was handed to her and somehow found herself outside, collecting her few belongings from the shack where the women took their midday meal and leaving the precincts of the mine under the bemused gaze of her workmates.

'Hannah! Hannah, wait! Where are you off too?' called out Maisie, pausing from her labours.

'Get on with your work, wench,' the foreman ordered the girl.

In turmoil Hannah swept on through the gateway and headed off down the road. She was back at the beginning with no work — and, worse, a black mark against her name! Or so it would appear. Surely, she reasoned, once her employer had checked the books himself he would find her innocent and review the situation? Then the small flare of hope spluttered and died. Hannah had not missed the gleam in the woman's eye as she had handed over her replacement's final wage. It had verged on the malicious.

What had she done to spark such plain dislike? Her only fault as far as she could make out was in complying with the mine owner's request to take temporary control of the vacancy at the office — and at his insistence, she might add. She recollected how she had resisted at first, instinct warning that this could be dangerous practice. Reflecting on how her mother had maintained that a person should always listen to their inner voice, Hannah thought how right she had been.

Troubled, deploring the unjust stain upon her character, Hannah pulled her shawl around her against the beating April rain and sped homewards as fast as her feet would take her.

5

'Madge, I didn't steal the money! I didn't!' Hannah said fiercely, colour rising in her cheeks.

Vinnie, sensing her mother's distress, stuffed her fist in her mouth, her round rosy face puckering, and Madge swept the child up into her arms before replying. 'It's all right, my lamb. Don't cry. Be a brave girl for Auntie Madge.' She shot Hannah a look. 'What? Hannah Morgan, tampering with the books and pocketing the difference? The very idea! Of course you wouldn't do anything so wicked. You're as honest as the day.'

Hannah took off her. sodden shawl, flung it to drip over the clothes-rail above the fire and sank miserably down on the stool. 'Madge, I don't understand it. I had every respect for Mr Prosser and I thought it was returned.

We were getting on so well.' She recollected how readily he'd given her the anthology of Mr Tennyson's verse. They had discovered shared favourites and he'd since loaned her other books. What could have taken place that had shaken that faith so implicitly? 'I thought he trusted me. He did trust me. He should know I would never do what he accused me of. Could Miss Black have been mistaken?'

Madge gave her lips a grim quirk. 'Call me an old cynic but it could be a case of jealousy winking its little green eye. If gossip is to be believed, Felicia Black has always carried a candle for Prosser. Put yourself in her position. She's no beauty; never was even as a girl. She gets confined to the house with an injury and the man of her dreams takes on an attractive young woman as a replacement. Not only is the new office assistant good to look upon, she's got a lively mind too . . . and Prosser would admire that. From what you've said, he's a great one for learning. I can't see Felicia Black coming up to expectations there.'

'And you think I do?'

Madge hinted a smile. 'I suspect if life had been kinder, you could have gone far, Hannah.'

'Life isn't kind. It's cruel and unfair. A child soon learns that.' Hannah swallowed down the lump that had risen to her throat. 'Madge, what am I to do? No job of work, no references. Labouring on the mine face was cheerless and hateful but it was better that than nothing, and you know what it was like when I looked for employment before. This time it will be worse. Word is bound to get out that I have been turned off with a black mark against my name.'

Madge, rocking the child, considered the dilemma. 'What if we waive the rental on your room for now and you help me on the holding? I know I said I wasn't in a position to take on paid labour but the situation has changed since then. I shall be starting the spring sowing any day, and my back isn't what it used to be. I'd be grateful for a young pair of hands to assist. You could take over the market stall for me as well; all that standing about is quite exhausting . . . and I'd not say no to some help about the house. There's no shortage of work at Brook Cottage, my girl,' Madge finished on a more encouraging note.

Hannah was silent. Appreciative though she was of her friend's offer, she knew that Madge was hardly in a position to support the three of them and though the rental would be a saving, she would still feel obliged to contribute something towards her own and Vinnie's keep. With a sinking heart she imagined her carefully hoarded money dwindling away.

'Madge, it's good of you and you know I'd do all I could to lighten your load, but it's earnings I need and I must find some paid work. Thinking back, didn't a farmer at one of the holdings say he could have a vacancy at some point in the spring? Middle Farm, I think it was.'

'That'll be Roland Prince's place. He's a hard taskmaster, Roland. Works his staff to the bone and makes no allowances for being female. Women toil all hours on his fields, soaked to the skin, covered head to foot with mud and worse. No, that's not for you.'

'It's no worse than the salt mine and I coped with that. Madge, I'm young and strong and I really am desperate. I'd agree to work day and night if it meant being paid for the privilege. Can you think where else I could approach?'

The child's eyes were now drooping, long lashes fanning her pink cheeks, and Madge settled her more comfortably in her arms while she gave the matter some thought. 'You'd really be best with a position in the town, wouldn't you? It isn't too far to travel and you'd get to know folks.'

'Malpas? I would not stand a chance there! I did not before, and I certainly won't now. Perhaps it is me. People there were so suspicious when I turned up that first day. It must simply be that sort of place.'

'Malpas is no different to any other town and I said at the time folks have to mind who they take into their homes. I shouldn't bother your head about that now. Things should be easier than it was.'

'Not if news of my dismissal gets out, it won't,' Hannah said. 'And get out it will if Miss Black has anything to do with it. I do not think she ever did like me. You were right on that score.'

'Hannah my love, if folk believe her they'll believe anything. Try not to worry. When one door closes another opens, as my mother used to say. There'll be a place for you, somewhere. Why not enquire about another office job? If you're quick about it and get taken on before any of this can get out, you'd be sure to prove your worth and your new employer would see Prosser's move for what it is — a gross mishandling of justice.'

'I do not know that I want to do office work ever again after what's happened,' Hannah retorted bitterly.

'No, I can understand it.' Madge regarded Hannah fondly. 'Look, my love. Why not leave it a while? Let the dust settle. Help me here on the holding. There's always something new to set the tongues wagging. Happen you could try again when all this has died down.'

Madge's reasoning made perfect sense and with a heavy heart Hannah gave in.

⋆ ⋆ ⋆

For the next weeks Hannah threw her energies into Brook Cottage. She drove the pony and trap to the merchant's for fodder for the stock, and into town to attend to the shopping. Once, while she was there, she took the opportunity to pay another visit to the churchyard for a more thorough investigation of the graves. Time had not allowed it before, and she felt a resurgence of interest as she made her way purposefully up the narrow street to where St Oswald's sat on its high hill.

Search though she might, she could find no Carraways at all interred there, a fact she found puzzling. Where then, was the resting place of the great-aunt who was her namesake? Where did her grandparents and other family members lie? It was a mystery and she stood there, a little frown on her brow, trying to figure out a solution to the conundrum.

Could her mother have been romancing when she had spoken of the place of which she had held such fond memories? It crossed Hannah's mind that her mother may not have lived here at all and the tales she had grown up with were nothing more than fabrication; pipe dreams to brighten a drab and wearying style of life. The notion, however, was dismissed the moment it was aired. Alice Bryson, nee Carraway, had been accepted by all who knew her to be unfailingly honourable in every way. She would never have stooped to any such thing and besides, there were landmarks here that Hannah recognised from her mother's reminiscences, indicating that she had known the area well. No, there had to be another explanation.

A cool wind whispered through the boughs of the churchyard yews that protected the sleepers, ruffling the grass, tugging at Hannah's shawl and blowing a strand of hair across her face. Impatiently she brushed it back, a little shiver touching her. She readjusted her shawl and flung a final glance around, satisfied that there was nothing here to suggest that her forbearers had existed in this tucked-away town on the borders of Wales.

She was about to leave when a voice hailed her. 'Hello, lady? You look a mite troubled. Is there ought can be done to help?'

Hannah started. Unbeknown to her, the young man who kept the graveyard tidy had entered the area and was standing before her, scythe over his shoulder.

'Oh, thank you, but I do not think so. I . . . I was just . . . looking for a name.'

'What would that be, then?'

'Carraway,' Hannah blurted. 'It was . . . it was the name of someone I knew.'

The fellow considered, and then shook his head. ''Tis not a local name, I'm thinking. There's no one here called Carraway and I know every stone like the back of my hand. Happen your acquaintance lies elsewhere.'

'Yes, you could be right,' Hannah said, and sending him a smile she left that quiet place and returned to the hurly-burly of the main street to deal with the shopping.

Very gradually life settled into a routine. Each day Hannah worked alongside Madge Nightingale, forking the over-winter ground, sowing the new seed and setting the tender young plants brought on in the cold frames. She tended the two cows that had both produced calves and were once more in milk. She herded the goats, fed the swine and saw to the fowl. With the advent of spring, the hens had come on lay again and there were eggs to collect and sort for market. Every Friday, no matter how many long hours she had put in on the holding, Hannah dipped into the purse that held her savings and counted out her keep for herself and her child, placing the precious coins in the battered tea-tin on the mantel in which Madge kept the household cash.

With the bulk of the work taken off her hands, Madge was often heard to lament that she was all but redundant, but the words were lightly spoken and she gladly spent her newly-acquired time with the child she had grown to love, playing tirelessly with her and keeping her occupied . . . which Hannah appreciated, for the little girl was becoming more of a handful.

'Eyes in the back of the head you need with our Vinnie!' Madge said one May evening. 'She slipped my attention this morning and do you know where I found her? In the hen-cote, talking nineteen-to-the-dozen to that flighty red hen she's taken a shine to! Well, talking in her little way. I swear the creature understands her baby-babble. It talks back to her. Vinnie's got a way with animals.'

'She's growing up a country girl. That's no bad thing, Madge dear. I wouldn't have it any other way.'

'Wouldn't you?' Madge went suddenly serious. 'I wish you would get out more, Hannah. Go to the chapel, get to know people. There'll be a young fellow somewhere who'll make you a good husband and be a father to the child.'

'Fiddle! I've said this before — Vinnie and I are happy as we are, so let's hear no more.' A smile took the sting out of Hannah's words. She went for a swift change of subject. 'Have you seen how the beans are coming on? More of this fine weather and we could have a bumper crop.'

* * *

One warm Sunday morning, with Madge gone to chapel, Hannah was seeing to the animals whilst keeping a watchful eye on her daughter. The child was cutting a back tooth and had been wakeful in the night and Hannah, having had little sleep, yawned widely as she went about the chores.

'Shall we have a little nap afterwards?' she said to the infant, who nodded and explored the offending gum with a small finger. The sight of the inflamed and swollen cheek tore at Hannah's heart and she bent to kiss her child. 'Naughty tooth, to give Vinnie so much trouble, isn't it? See, here's your little hen come to say how sorry for you she is.'

Distracted, Vinnie babbled something unintelligible to the bird and tried to stroke it, but the hen went squawking off and the child's face crumpled. 'Never mind,' Hannah said hastily. 'Shall we get a drink? Wouldn't you like some of that nice lemon cordial that Mama made for Vinnie?'

From the jug in the scullery she poured the drinks and took the cups outside, settling down with her daughter under the blossoming pear tree to sip and relax a little. Soon the child was nodding off in her arms and Hannah took the opportunity to close her own stinging eyes and rest them . . .

6

'Auntannie! Auntannie! Look at me. Look at me . . . e!' The child squeals with delight.

The cottage door is open to the summer's day and the two women come hurrying out, crossing the yard to stand under the pear tree and gaze around them in bemusement.

'Child, where are you?' the cobbler's wife calls out anxiously, looking over the yard.

'I's hiding.' A delighted giggle sounds from somewhere above their heads. 'I's in the pear twee. Look up here. Look at me, Auntannie!'

They look up into the spreading boughs and the laughter comes again.

'Niece.' The other woman looks shocked. 'What in the world are you doing up there? Have I not told you often enough what unseemly behaviour

111

it is for little girls to climb trees? What if you should fall?'

'I won't. An' I's not a'seemly, not wealy. I's a good girl, I is. I's clever.'

The cobbler's wife turns away to hide a smile.

The faintest glimmer of amusement also appears on her companion's rather austere face. She shakes her head in reproof. 'What a little hoyden! I think you're getting a tad too clever for your own good. There are times when I truly think you should have been born a boy. Come along down from there now, before you fall and hurt yourself.'

'Must I, Auntannie? I like it here. It's all gween and cool.'

'Green,' she corrects. 'Grrrr . . . een. Try rolling your r's.'

'Can't.'

The cobbler's wife steps in to bring the child out of the tree. 'Come along down before you take a tumble. Come on, there's a good girl. Come with Madge and see your kitten. She's ready to come home with you now . . . unless of course you have changed your mind and don't want her any more?'

The ploy works. There is a rustling of branches, a small shower of leaves and two stick-thin, pantalooned legs appear. 'Catch me! Catch me!'

Both reach up and between them the women bring the wriggling bundle to safety.

'Now can I see my kitten?'

'Please!' the aunt corrects on a sigh. 'May I see my kitten, please. Manners, child. A good girl always remembers to say please and thank you.'

'I does. I is good, isn't I, Mistwess Nightinfing?'

'There then, that's a hard old name for a young tongue to get itself round, isn't it?' The cobbler's wife coaxes the child. 'Why not call me Auntie Madge, like I've told you before?'

'Auntie Madge, may I see my kitten, PWEASE?'

'Bless you, child, of course you shall. She's in the stable with her little brother and sister.' The cobbler's wife beams a smile. 'Hold my hand, there's a good girl. That's right. Let's go and look. Have you thought of a name for her yet?'

'No. I can't fink.'

'What about Tibby? We had a cat here called Tibby at one time. Sweet as nines, she was. She was a tabby, too.'

'Tibby. Yes, I can say that pwoperly, can't I? Shall we call the kitten Tibby, Auntannie?'

'As you wish. Yes, Tibby will do perfectly.'

The little girl breaks away again, and laughing and clapping her hands together in excitement she goes scampering on ahead of the older women in the direction of the wooden outbuildings. 'Tibby! I's coming! Come on, Auntie Madge . . .'

* * *

'Annie!' Hannah exclaimed, waking abruptly with the name on her lips. For once she had retained the name of one of her dream people! It wasn't much of a way forward, and yet Hannah had the sense of getting somewhere at last.

Vinnie was still sleeping, thumb plugged in her mouth, but Hannah had cramp in the arm that supported the child and she cautiously eased it away, leaning back against the knobbly trunk of the tree.

The scent of blossom wafted, sweet, evocative, and for once Hannah felt at peace with life and gave her tired mind up to enjoying the dappled sunlight that slanted through the branches of the tree and to listening to the song of a blackbird. That was how Madge found them on her return.

'Bless the child,' she whispered, plumping down on the low bench that Judd Nightingale had made beneath the tree. She put aside her prayer book and loosened her heavy woollen coat. 'Ah, that's better. Warm for the time of year, isn't it? Look at our Vinnie. Is the tooth through yet?'

'I think so. She won't let me look.

Did she keep you awake in the night, Madge? She was crying a lot. I had to come down and make a warm drink to help settle her.'

'I did rouse once but I soon dropped off again. What about you? There are dark shadows under your eyes. You had little rest yourself last night, I'm thinking.'

'Well, no. I fell asleep just before — not like me to nap during the day.' Hannah hesitated, wondering whether to continue, and then took the plunge. 'Madge, do you remember my once asking you if you dreamed much? You said it was commonplace to dream but there is nothing commonplace about mine.'

'Yes, I remember. You weren't dreaming of my Judd again?'

'No, it was not that this time. This was the visitor with the small girl. I think I mentioned them last time. Aunt Annie, she calls the woman. Did you ever know anyone of that name?'

Madge was looking altogether uneasy

and it occurred to Hannah that if her friend had been of any other persuasion rather than the staunch Methodist she was, she may have resorted to crossing herself to ward off some unwelcome presence in her midst.

'Bless you, daughter,' Madge said. 'I've known many an Annie over the years. There was Annie Dyke, she's Annie Chidlow now. Annie Waters, Annie Farley. It could have been any one of these. But listen to me, Hannah,' she said, moistening her lips. 'I should forget these dreams. They're nothing but muddled thoughts we get when our minds are not settled . . . or in my case when I've had strong cheese for supper. It always makes me dream, does cheese.' She rose to her feet. 'Cup of tea? I'm spitting feathers. The parson didn't half go on this morning. I thought the sermon would never end.'

Absently Hannah watched Madge cross the yard with her nimble, surprisingly youthful stride, and disappear into the cottage. Her mind was still on that uncanny peephole into the past. *Annie,* she thought. *Who could she have been, the stiffly-laced woman in outdated black bombazine? Who was the little girl who led her aunt such a merry dance?*

Vinnie chose that moment to stir and Hannah sighed and reluctantly turned her attention back to the present.

*   *   *

May came in, gloriously blue and gold, with lengthening days and spells of sunshine and showers that spurred a growth of weeds, bringing ever more work on the land.

Hannah tackled it stoically, grubbing out the unwelcome growth to give her young plantlets the space to grow strong. Indoors, she swept and scrubbed and even treated the smoke-grimed walls to a freshening coat of whitewash.

'Daughter, you'll wear yourself out with all this,' Madge said, coming in one day to find Hannah up a stepladder, applying a strong-smelling layer of tar to the ceiling beams.

She had wound a length of cloth round her head to protect her hair from splashes and wore an old working smock of Judd Nightingale's over her clothes. Nonetheless, her hands and upper arms bore clear evidence of her labours and Madge clucked her tongue in reproof.

'Look at you! Have a care you don't burn yourself. That tar is nasty stuff, Hannah. There's some of my marigold salve on the shelf. Mind you dab some on when you're done. Tarring the ceiling, indeed! Whatever next, I wonder?'

'It needed doing and I found the barrel of tar in the lean-to so I thought I'd put it to good use. There's beetles at work in these rafters. Look at all the holes.'

'Fie, that's nothing new! The place hasn't fallen apart yet and it won't for many a year to come ... but there, don't think I don't appreciate what you're doing. I do. You're the daughter I never had and I bless the day the Lord guided you to my door.' She broke off, clearly trying to frame her next words, her head characteristically posed. 'Hannah, I've been thinking. I feel I shouldn't take your money off you for food. Mercy me, you work hard enough here as it is and anyway, you don't eat enough to keep a sparrow alive and what Vinnie has is next to nothing. Let's leave it for now, shall we?'

Hannah put down the tar-brush. 'Not pay for our keep? That's kind of you but I could not. You rely on it too much.'

The small luxuries that appeared from time to time had not escaped her notice; thicker curtains at the door and windows to keep out the draughts, coal in the shed to supplement the supply of logs for the fire, a new cooking pot, even a vase for the dresser, cheap but cheerful. Minor things, and yet it made a difference to the general comfort and wellbeing and Hannah was filled with approval that her friend should invest her extra pennies in this way. Madge, however, accustomed to a widowhood of make-do-and-mend, looked a little sheepish at being caught out.

'Well now, I allow I have made things a tad cosier.'

'And will continue to have the means to do so,' Hannah said stoutly. 'Madge, my mind is made up. Anyway, summer is almost here. There'll be hay that needs turning, amongst other things. Farmers must be taking on extra labour now. I might go along to the farm I told you about and see if there's any work to be had. You never know, they may be glad of an extra milkmaid or someone to work in the dairy, I'd take on any work.'

'Are we talking about Middle Farm?' Madge looked grim. 'Extra slave labour, you mean! But have it your own way. I know when your mind is made up — and just when I was thinking how grand it was to be producing quite a bit more on the holding than previously. That's due to your assistance. It's paying dividends, Hannah. Just remember there's always a place for you here at Brook Cottage.'

★   ★   ★

'You're too late,' Roland Prince said. He was a small, spare man, sallow-faced and sharp-featured, putting Hannah in mind of a weasel. 'I've taken on all the female labour I need right now. Pity you didn't come a couple of weeks ago.'

'I was going to but I couldn't spare the time, what with all the hoeing that was needed. The weeds sprang up overnight after those showers of rain we had. It was all I could do to keep on top of it all.'

'Aye, it's true. Weeds always do present a problem this time of year. I've heard what a good worker you are. Widow Nightingale's struck lucky there. Why are you leaving?'

'I'm not. I just need a regular job of work. I don't mind helping in the farmhouse. Anything, really. Even part-time would be better than nothing. In fact it might be no bad thing. I could keep up with what I do at Brook Cottage then.'

'Part-timers are no good to me and the missus copes well enough in the house. I've daughters to lend a hand, when they'll get up off their lazy backsides, that is.' He shot the half-filled tumbrel cart he was loading up with manure a glance. 'Got to get on. Time's money, is it not? Sorry I can't oblige. I know a genuine worker when I see one an' all.'

Hannah had been almost sure of obtaining a place here and being turned away was crushing. Giving the matter some thought she decided to call at the next holding, a smaller place with a limited acreage, managed by a youngish man and his wife.

The wife looked not far off giving

123

birth and Hannah's spirits rose a little at the prospect that they might need help.

'Work?' The farmer scratched his head. 'I dunno, missus. Getting in paid labour isn't something I've ever considered, to be honest with you.'

'You may soon need someone,' Hannah said with a pointed glance at the fresh-faced young woman who was pegging out washing on the line.

'Oh, my Dora's strong as an ox. Says her ma had her babes like shelling peas and she's no reason to think she'll be any different herself. Then again, I will bear it in mind.'

'I'm willing to do anything. Work on the fields, scrub the yards, see to the animals. I'd muck out the byre if need be.'

'That's good to know. Meantime, we're managing. Sorry, though. Try the Alport. It's a bigger set-up than here and it's nice and up-to-date, too. Happen they'll want help in the dairy.'

'I'll do that,' Hannah said, not with

any great confidence.

Farmer Marsh of the Alport was known throughout the district to be a fair and just employer. Work at his establishment was hugely sought after and once taken on, a member of staff rarely left. Trying not to dwell on the risk of having her hopes dashed again, she headed off along the grassy lane to where the farm sat amongst spruce new barns.

It was as she suspected. The Alport ran its full quota of staff and there was no knowledge of anyone leaving in the foreseeable future. The same went for the rest of the larger holdings she tried on the heath. It was a sad case of history repeating itself. No one wanted a milkmaid or dairymaid. Neither did any of the farmhouses have a vacancy for indoor staff. No sooner did a position come available, explained a buxom wife with florid cheeks and a brood of children peeping out from behind her skirts, than it was snapped up by a local girl, often a younger sister of an established member of the staff.

'That way, folks know they're trustworthy!' the woman finished with a nod that said all.

Having suffered enough humiliation, Hannah gave herself pause for thought. Plainly word of her disgrace had not only spread amongst the farming fraternity but was taking a while to be forgotten and done with.

She tried another tack. Household laundry in the more affluent homes of the district was tackled by a brawny-armed woman and her two daughters from Oldcastle, a mile or two on from Cuddington. They'd travel with a donkey and cart, collecting the dirty washing and delivering it a week later washed, starched, pressed and pristine.

Hannah waylaid a grubby-faced goose-girl with a flapping herd of snowy-plumaged birds. 'Excuse me. Do you know if the washer-wife might want a helper?'

'Hattie Grimble? I shouldn't think so.

They seem to manage well enough between them. Was it work that you wanted? I reckon there's no harm in enquiring.'

'Could you point me the way?'

Her route led back across the heath along lanes that dipped between high banks. It was late May now and hedgerows frothed with colourful blossom. Birds sang joyfully and the air was full of the scent of midsummer, but for once Hannah was blind and deaf to the richness of her surroundings. All she could think of was the pressing need to find work. Her money would not last forever and despite Madge's assurances to the contrary she could hardly impose upon her friend's hospitality and good nature indefinitely.

All at once the sheer hopelessness of it all was too much to bear, and a black fog of despair swept over her, deep and unyielding. There and then in the middle of the lane Hannah put her face in her hands and gave in to a violent storm of weeping. How long it lasted she had no idea. On and on went the gulping sobs, despair flooding through her.

She was snapped abruptly out of her misery by the clamour of galloping hooves. Through a blur of tears she saw coming towards her at full pelt the unwelcome shape of a riderless horse. Its head was high, its mane streaming and tail thrashing, and a broken rein was in danger of getting entangled in the animal's legs and bringing it down. For a heart-stopping moment Hannah was powerless to move. With a terrible sense of inevitability she watched the runaway coming closer and closer, threatening to bear down on her and end her troubles for good!

7

'Stop! Who . . . oa,' she commanded. 'Whoa there!' The stench of sweating horseflesh assailed her nostrils; there was a frightened snorting and a scupper of hooves and the horse checked in front of her and slithered to a stop. It stood a moment, looking at her warily through eyes that rolled whitely in alarm. Right at the last minute some vital sense of self-preservation had struck her. Summoning all her willpower she planted herself more firmly on the path and stretched out her arms, standing her ground fearlessly in the way she had seen of horsemen in the past.

'Whoa, then. Steady,' Hannah said in soothing tones. 'Good boy. Let me catch hold of your bridle. There. Well, look at you. What a state you're in.'

The horse was blowing; foam

dripped from its nostrils and the bright chestnut coat was lathered and dark with sweat. Crooning to it all the while, Hannah glanced around her. There had to be a rider here somewhere. Problem was, where?

'What am I going to do with you?' she said aloud.

No sooner were the words out than she spotted in the distance a limping figure and clicking her tongue to the horse she set off towards it. The figure seemed familiar; Hannah recognised the eldest son from the mill with his shock of auburn hair. Telltale grass-bits clung to his clothes and he looked dazed and slightly abashed, but he managed a smile as he took the horse from her.

'Mistress, you've done me a good turn. Our Will would never have forgiven me if I had gone back without the horse. How can I ever begin to thank you?' His rumbling country voice was strangely comforting.

'I need no thanks, sir. I am only too

glad to have been of help. The rein was broken. It could have caused mischief and I would not have wanted to see the animal hurt.'

'You're a brave lady. It takes spirit to do what you did.'

'I just didn't stop to think. He seemed relieved to be caught . . . But sir, you look shaken. Are you all right?' she asked.

'I will be in a moment or two. Tough as old boots, I am. I must have bumped my head when I came off.' Swaying a little, he fingered the back of his skull, wincing. 'Well bless me, if there isn't a lump there as big as an egg. Needless to say I'm no rider. Our Will is the horseman of the family. He buys horses from the sale that other folks won't entertain and next minute has them eating out of his hand.' He rubbed his face bemusedly with his fist, smiling down at her from his great height.

When Hannah had first come across Cameron Blake, she had found the burly frame, flaming thatch of hair and bushy beard a little frightening. Now, she saw how kind the speaker's eyes were; how they twinkled with good humour and how engaging his smile was. She also noticed with concern how pale and drawn his face currently appeared.

'Sir, you took a nasty tumble. I think you should sit down quietly for a little while and recover. Let me hold the horse. See, he's quite happy eating the grass.'

For a moment she thought he would brush her words aside, but then plainly thinking the better of it Cameron Blake relinquished the reins and subsided thankfully amongst the foaming spears of meadowsweet of the bank. 'Ah, that's better. I'll admit the world was spinning a bit.' He shrugged his massive shoulders and squinted across at her.

'You must be Widow Nightingale's lodger. Haven't I seen you in the town before?'

'Yes, you will have, sir. I'm Hannah

Morgan,' she replied with caution in her voice.

'Someone said you worked at the salt mine.'

'Not any more. There was a . . . a parting of the ways. It's a wonder you haven't heard. Everyone else seems to have.'

He looked at her blankly, and then clapped a hand across his forehead. 'Oh, forgive me, clumsy fool that I am. The fellow turned you off, didn't he? Some misunderstanding in the office.'

'That is a commendably tactful way of putting it, sir, but I can assure you that I did no wrong.' To her chagrin Hannah felt her eyes again filling up with tears. Never would she forget the shame and humiliation of the false accusation and it took little to bring the event back in all its painful detail.

Cameron Blake's face softened. 'There now, I've upset you. Seems you've been through a hard time, ma'am. I'm not going anywhere just yet and folks say I'm a good listener, if you'd care to talk about it.'

Hannah hesitated, but his concern seemed so genuine and she felt in such low spirits that she shrugged doubt aside and launched into what had happened, haltingly at first, then gaining impetus, the words tumbling from her lips as mingled indignation and despondency were given voice.

She told him about Prosser's apparent interest in her, his geniality and the abrupt withdrawal of faith when the assistant had made her supposed discovery.

'Miss Black had to have been in error. I had checked my figures thoroughly and I know they were not incorrect. I would never short-change my employer. It would simply not enter my head to do such an awful thing.'

'No, I don't believe it would. You've too honest a face for that. Was the lost money ever found?'

'I do not know. I was sent off straight away and I have heard nothing since. Most likely they think I have kept it for myself — as if I would!'

Hannah fumbled in her pocket for a kerchief and blew her nose. 'What a silly you must think me, blubbering like a baby, but it was so unfair and now I cannot get work anywhere. People are either full up or they have heard what happened and won't take me on. I have a child to bring up. Without a regular wage I do not know how I shall manage.'

'It's a pretty pickle and no mistake. Is that what you are about today? Calling at places for work?'

She mopped her damp cheeks fiercely. 'Yes, I was on my way to see the washer-wife. I thought I might strike lucky there.'

'Hattie Grimble? Not a chance! She's got those wenches of hers to do all the pounding and soaping. Besides, I reckon you can do better than that.' He gazed at her, his eyes intensely blue in his rugged face. 'Father was only saying a few nights ago how we could do with someone at the mill to tidy the place up and see after us all.'

'A housekeeper, you mean?'

'That's right. It's been a while since the millhouse had a mistress. Mother's been gone these fifteen years. Will was nobbut a babe in the cradle. 'Twas the bad winter took her off. She caught bronchitis and it turned to pneumonia.'

'What a tragedy. Who looked after your baby brother?'

'Father got a woman from the village to come and live in, but as soon as Will was able to fend for himself she left to get wed. We've had others since, come to clean and cook and what have you. None of them stayed.'

Hannah's mind raced. Cleaning and cooking for a family of menfolk seemed a simple matter to her. 'Do you suppose your father would take me on?' she asked, hope blazing on her face. 'I'd do my best to please.'

Again the smile, warm, broader this time. 'Well now, I reckon I owe you a favour. If you hadn't caught this horse there's a chance it would be in the next county by now. What if you come back with me and wait while I speak with Father?'

Hannah could hardly believe her ears. 'Are you sure?'

'Aye, of course I am. Happen it's meant, you coming along at that moment.'

'I don't know about that,' Hannah said. She looked at him with concern. 'Do take your time. A blow to the head is not a thing to be taken lightly.'

'Oh, I'm feeling better by the minute and my brother will be wondering about the horse. I only borrowed it to deliver a message to the Alport. A bird flew out of the hedge and startled it. Will said to be on my guard.'

He pulled himself to his feet, swaying slightly, steadying. He was indeed looking better, Hannah thought. The colour had returned to his face and his voice was stronger.

Slowly they set off, the horse plodding behind, sobered now and contrite. After a while they reached the mill, standing back off its cobbled forecourt. Beside it stood the millhouse and Hannah gave it an interested glance. A sturdy structure of locally sourced red stone, it had a blue-tiled roof and a tall chimney on either end. There was a weedy garden and an orchard of hard and soft fruit trees, all bearing. Stabling and a range of outbuildings built of the same stone as the house flanked a small yard and there was a field where the mill-horse grazed. Hannah liked the look of the place. Behind her back, her fingers were soundly crossed.

Cameron handed the animal over to a tall lad whom Hannah took to be the brother, giving a brief explanation as to what had happened. The lad shot Hannah no more than a cursory look before leading the horse into the stable, where he could be heard whistling through his teeth as he checked the chestnut over for injury.

Fetching Hannah a wink of encouragement, Cameron left her to wait by the millrace and disappeared through a side entrance of the mill into what looked like office premises, shutting the door behind him.

Time ticked by. Hannah, watching the water run deep and green, wondered what was happening between father and son. Every now and then she threw the mill-office a glance. Voices issued from an open window but because of the clamour of the millwheel and the noisy thrash of water, it was impossible to make out what was being said. Presently the door opened and Miller Blake emerged, together with his son.

'Mistress Morgan? I'm Jack Blake.' The miller stood a head shorter than his lad but he was still a strapping figure of a man. Mill-dust powdered his grizzled head and he wheezed a little, as if the flour was permanently lodged in his lungs. Despite that, a degree of humour lurked in the grey-blue gaze and tugged at the corners of his mouth. 'Pleased to meet you, ma'am. My boy tells me you are looking for a position.'

'Yes sir,' Hannah answered in a low voice. Fear at rejection dried her throat and she cleared it nervously.

'You worked at Lower Dirtwich, I believe.'

'Yes sir.'

'And got turned off. Some confusion over the book-keeping, it appears.'

'Sir, there was no dishonesty on my part. I swear it.'

'Aye, well, Prosser always was over-hasty. If all was innocent and above board and, from what my boy here says, there's no reason to suspect that it wasn't, happen the man will most likely come to his senses and ask you back. What then?'

'I'd be inclined to turn him down — particularly if I'd had a more suitable offer,' Hannah said, suddenly finding her spirit.

The miller gave a splutter of wheezy laughter. 'That's what I like to hear, that is; a person who can speak up for herself. Blow me, yes! You have an honest stamp. It's written all over you and I pride myself on being a judge of character. Well then, mistress, what do you say to housekeeping for a bevy of menfolk? We're a rough and ready crew and it's a mite isolated here, you understand. Others have found it lonesome.'

'That would not be a problem to me. I should imagine there would be plenty to keep one occupied. I'd give it my best, miller.'

'Yes, I rather think you would. A month's trial might be no bad thing. No bad thing at all. After that — well, we'll see. 'Twould be live-in, mind.'

'Live-in?' Hannah's hopes plummeted.

'We've had housekeepers on a daily basis before and it's never worked out. Well, there's the trudge from home in the morning and back again at night. It's no easy step from the town or wherever, especially in the dark of winter.'

'It's no different to walking to the salt

mine.' Hannah was quick to fight her corner. 'I cannot say that ever bothered me. I quickly grew used to it.'

'That's as maybe but it'll not change my mind. If you want the position you'll have to live in the house with us.'

Hannah's bottom lip trembled. 'Sir, I have a child.'

'Aye, I'd heard as much — a babe, coming up to an age for getting into mischief. A grain mill is no place for children. 'Tis too dangerous, what with the millrace and the wheel turning, not to mention the drop from the grain hatch. No, mistress. I'd not feel easy. Best you foster the infant out. There's plenty of women will take on a child alongside their own.'

'But, sir . . . '

'No buts. You'd need to watch your little'n all the time and at the expense of your duties. No, the offer's there but on this I stand firm. I remember how it was when my boys were small. Run off her feet, my good wife was. No, we don't want any mishaps here.'

Hannah stared at him, her mind in turmoil. She could not argue with his reasoning. Many were the times Madge had uttered the very same words. However, the thought of being parted from her child was heart-wrenching. Vinnie might forget who she was! That would be hard to bear.

'Look,' the miller said, quite kindly. 'Why not ask Widow Nightingale if she'll do the honours? She's done it up to now, hasn't she? I'd not object to your slipping out to see your little'n now and again. I know how it is with women and their childer and I'd not be labelled unkind.'

Hannah thought fast. It wasn't only Vinnie. Her room under the eves of Brook Cottage had become a safe haven in a hard and insecure world, and Madge was a good friend. She didn't want to leave her lodgings, much less relinquish Vinnie into permanent fostering, but what choice had she?

'Madge will take Vinnie in, I am almost sure of it,' she said in a voice that trembled. 'Thank you, miller. All being well I shall be pleased to come and work for you.'

'That's settled then. You'll find the millhouse no palace. It lacks a woman's touch. Still, I daresay you'll see what needs doing. As to wages, I'll give you three shillings and sixpence per week all found. A month's trial, and if we suit each other the job is yours for keeps. What do you say?'

It was much more generous than her pay at the mine office and to Hannah it felt like riches. Bar Vinnie's fostering fees, she would have few other outgoings and would soon replenish her depleted savings.

Hannah took the large hand the miller extended and the matter was sealed.

★ ★ ★

The attic bedroom which Hannah was allocated was airy and bright. With the floor swept and a duster flourished over the solid country furniture, the bed made up with surprisingly good linen from an oaken press on the landing, Hannah had no complaints of what was to be her future sanctuary.

As to the rest of the house, lacking a woman's touch indeed! Windows that should have sparkled in the sunlight were thick with grime, and the flour-dust that flew from the clothes of the men lay thickly on every surface. Ancient cobwebs laced the rafters overhead and there was evidence of vermin in the larder. The flagged floor of the big kitchen was indescribably filthy. A deep brownstone sink under the window was heaped with unwashed dishes, as was the deal table that had not received a scrubbing in many a day.

The boys' rooms — Miller Blake generally referred to his sons as 'the boys', Hannah learned, though Cameron and Thomas were grown men and Will was fast catching up with them — had to be seen to be believed. Unwashed bedding gave off a sour smell and dirty clothes lay everywhere, all crusted with the same ubiquitous dust from the mill.

Shaking her head wordlessly at the blatant disregard of a house that must once have been a comfortable home, Hannah rolled up her sleeves and set to work, starting in the kitchen where most of the living was done. For a full day she scrubbed and scoured, and went on to wage war on the cobwebs throughout the rest of the house. She beeswaxed the planked floors and furniture, and by the end of the week the place was looking, if not exactly palatial, at least a good deal more presentable and smelling sweeter than before.

She liked the small front parlour that had been furnished with such care ... that is, she liked all but the horsehair sofa that prickled interminably when sat upon.

A little half-grown cat, acquired from Alport Farm, dealt with the vermin. Another week went by and Hannah, aching with the loss of her child, plucked up the courage to request permission to go and see her and was told to do so as and when she felt fit, an instruction which eased her mind considerably.

As she went upon her duties she could hear Cameron's rich baritone, singing the old songs as he loaded up the cart. She found the work no harder than the mine, the company a good deal more genial and, pleasingly tired after her toils, Hannah fell into bed at night and slept soundly till morning.

At least, that could be said of most nights. There were others when the dreams returned; real, vivid.

8

'The millwheel! The millwheel! I want to see it now, Auntannie. Please can I?'

'Yes, of course. You must hold my hand, though. The water is deep just here.'

Woman and child mount the bridge and stand there, watching the wheel churn up the water below into a torrent of green, sunlight catching the spray in myriad flashes of colour.

'How does it work, Auntannie? How does it make the flour? Tell me!'

'Child, child, you and your questions. There's another wheel inside the mill and machinery with cogs and pistons. You've seen the great millstones? Well, the grains fall between them and get ground up into flour.'

'And then we make bwead with it.'

'That's right. Clever girl. Shall we go in and see the miller?'

'Oh yes, yes! Will Master Bertie be there, Auntannie? I like Master Bertie.'

'Because he always has a comfit for you in his pocket, I'm thinking. No, child. I fear you are to be disappointed. Master Bertie has gone away on his ship. Remember me telling you how he sails the seas for weeks on end?'

'Mmm.' The little girl is crestfallen. 'Why does he?'

'It is his living. Some men are millers, others are farmers and some are cobblers like Master Nightingale.'

'What about my papa? What does he do?'

The aunt's lips tighten. 'Sweetheart, if I could answer that I would. Perhaps he works in an office and wears a white collar. You'd like that, wouldn't you?'

'Yes. But I wish Master Bertie was here.'

★ ★ ★

Across the way the millwheel creaked and thrashed, drowning out the voices

149

in her head. Hannah's eyes fluttered open. Heavy rain hammered against the bedroom window; the millrace was in full spate.

'The dream again,' Hannah murmured. Lulled by the beating raindrops she gave herself up again to sleep.

★　★　★

'You're a grand cook, Hannah,' Cameron said one evening as they sat at supper. Two generous portions of pudding had been made short work of. He put aside his empty plate with a sigh of deep contentment.

'I'll second that,' his father said from his place at the head of the table. 'My Tilda was a dab hand at apple sponge and that was every bit as good.'

'Thank you,' Hannah said. 'I came across the apples in the stable loft. They're good keepers, barely a bad one amongst them,' she added.

'They'd be out of the orchard. 'Twas my grandfather that planted it.'

'There is a vegetable patch as well but all gone to weed,' Hannah said. 'I thought I would tidy it up a bit.'

'Don't go mauling yourself about. I'll dig the ground over for you,' Cameron said at once.

'Oh, would you?' Hannah met his gaze in gratitude and her heart, absurdly, skipped a beat. She looked hastily away. 'It's not too late to grow a row of beans and put in some cabbages. Having one's own vegetables is better than buying them from the market. They're never entirely fresh. It's a saving, too.'

'Thrift, that's what I like to hear,' the miller said, eyes twinkling. 'Look after the pennies and the pounds look after themselves. Blow me, yes!'

Thomas fetched Hannah a wink. 'Let's have plum duff one night, Hannah. I'm partial to plum duff with a custard sauce.'

'You'll have to wait for the plums to ripen for that. There's a fine crop this year. I'll be able to bottle some for the winter. Likely you'll be tired of plum duff by spring.'

'Never,' Thomas said, grinning all over his good-looking face.

Purring before the fire was the little grey cat Hannah had obtained from Farmer Marsh. It had proved an inveterate ratter and had become a favourite with everyone.

Miller Blake helped himself to the last portion of apple sponge. 'Wouldn't like it to go to waste, you understand. Amazing, how you women can rustle up a meal out of a few scraps of this and that. I reckon you'll have learned it at your mother's knee, Hannah lass, same as my Tilda.'

He looked at Hannah with mild curiosity and three other pairs of eyes turned on her attentively. Any reference to Hannah's past seemed a source of interest to the Blakes and she felt herself quail before their collected gaze.

'Well, yes, and Madge Nightingale was a good example,' she replied, neatly steering the conversation away from what could have been troubled waters. She found a smile. 'Is everyone finished?' There was a murmur of assent and a few satisfied belches, and Hannah rose and began gathering up the dirty pots. 'There is cheese,' she offered. 'Would anyone like to finish their meal with some?'

'Aye!' they chorused to a man.

She disappeared into the larder and was soon back bearing a large wedge of red Cheshire, a dish of butter and some fresh-baked biscuits.

She went to the fire and poured tea from a big brown pot, and although the company had polished off a mutton pie the size of which had to be seen to be believed and a veritable mountain of mashed potato, followed by the pudding, they fell on the fare as if there was no tomorrow.

Hannah was astonished at the enjoyment to be had in shopping with a full purse, and this was not the only reason for her pleasure. Now that to all intent and purposes she was in employment at

153

the mill, all past discrepancies were forgotten, for people had every respect for Miller Blake and his sons. The town in the main was coming to accept Hannah's presence in their midst and on shopping excursions she looked forward to chatting to the shopkeepers and hearing their news about their nearest and dearest.

Preparing the meals in what was now a pristine and workable kitchen was more a delight than a chore. It was satisfying to see the Blakes gathered around the big deal table that was now scrubbed to a fierce whiteness. Topping it all, sitting down to eat with the family at the miller's insistence made her fee! gratifyingly like one of them.

* * *

The weather remained dry and Hannah was able to wash the bedding and every item of clothing she could lay her hands on. She cleaned the windows, swilled the pathways, took her mop and broom across to the mill and, clearing the matter with her employer who was in residence at the time, gave the mill-office a thorough sweeping, taking care not to disturb the papers that were lying everywhere in dusty piles.

Throughout the activity the miller sat chewing the end of his quill behind a battered desk that had probably been there since the mill was built in the mid-1600s.

'I've no head for reckoning,' Miller Blake said of a sudden, making her start. Gloomily he indicated the hard-backed ledger in front of him. 'I can do it at a push, and that's about it. My Tilda was a boon in the office, you understand, could add up a row of figures in a wink. Put me to shame, she did.'

Hannah was struck by a crippling sense of panic. The very mention of books and reckoning stirred bitter memories and going hot and cold by turn, she stood twisting the dusting-cloth helplessly in her hands.

No word had come that her dismissal from the mine had been a misapprehension and knowing Prosser as she did — his pride, the high-handedness she suspected stemmed from shame at his humble origins, and, yes, a male pig-headedness when it came to admitting he was wrong — she had not expected anything else.

'What I'm trying to say is this,' Miller Blake went on, seemingly unaware of Hannah's discomfort. 'Cameron tells me you have a good head for figures. Reckoned up a grocery list in a trice, he said, just like his ma used to. The other morning I heard you give a customer a total for his cart of grains. Aye, spot-on it was too.'

Hannah managed to collect her scattered wits. 'I'm sorry, Mr Blake. I should have called you straight away. I was in the forecourt alone and the man was in a hurry or I would have.'

'How did you know what to tell him?'

'I've watched the way Cameron and Thomas do it. It isn't difficult to size up a load and put a price on it, once you know the values.'

'That's commendable, that is. Hannah lass, do you realise your month's trial is up come Wednesday? You will be stopping on with us, won't you?'

'Of course I will. Do you know I hadn't given the time a thought? How it's flown.'

'Aye. That's settled then. There is one more thing.'

'Yes? Is something wrong?'

'Not with our new housekeeper, there isn't. Blow me, no. She couldn't be more right, she couldn't. No, it's this blitherin' figurin'!' He shuddered as if he had swallowed vinegar and stabbed a thumb irritably at the open ledger with its columns of crossings-out and blotches of ink. 'If you could spare an hour from all the sweepin' and titivatin', Hannah lass, I'd be grateful if you could pass an eye over these figures for me.'

Hannah's insides churned. She had

not been expecting this and she did not know what to say. 'Sir, I . . . I don't know if I can. It's . . . well . . . ' She stammered to a stop.

'It's all right, lass,' Miller Blake said. 'I've not forgotten about that spot of bother you had. It was tactless of me springing it on you like this. Figurin' and ledgers is bound to be a sensitive area, blow me, yes! Let's put it this way. I'm no fool. If I'd thought you a dubious prospect I'd not have taken you on in the first place, would I?'

'No, I suppose not.'

'We talked all that out when you came here looking for a position, didn't we?'

'Well, yes.'

'So what's the problem?'

'Sir, you don't understand. What happened was unjust.'

'Aye, I know, and these things go deep. Best you consign the whole unfortunate episode to the past, Hannah. We all have to do that at some point. You never move on if you let things eat you up.' He leaned closer. 'See here, I'll pay you an extra shilling a week if you'll book-keep for me. What my raddled old brain takes half a day to work out you'll likely do in minutes.'

'I don't think so.' Hannah allowed herself a small smile.

'There now, you should smile more often. It brightens the place up. Shall you oblige, then? I'd appreciate it more than I could say.'

Hannah gave in with a sigh. 'As you wish, though it might be best if someone checks the figures afterwards.'

'No need, I'm sure, but if you insist, Cameron will do it. 'Tis he who writes the letters to clients and makes out the bills. He's got a good head on his shoulders for all he's such a bear of a chap. If he wasn't needed in the mill I'd be more than happy for him to take over the office fully, but there 'tis.' Miller Blake nodded, well satisfied at the way things had gone, and slammed shut the offending account book. 'Well then, Hannah. I reckon fortune did me a good turn when you arrived on the doorstep.'

'Thank you, sir. It's good of you to say so. Now may I get on with my work?'

'Aye, off you go. Give us another smile first. That's it. What a sight for sore eyes.'

Warming to his attitude, her smile broadened. As she left her heart felt lighter than in a long while.

9

'But Father, I want to go to sea.' Thomas faced his father across the desk of the mill-office. 'I want to be like Great-Uncle Bertie and sail the world. Being homebound isn't for me. There's a whole lot going on out there. I want to be part of it.'

He flung out his hands beseechingly, withdrawing them in alarm as his father was taken by a spasm of coughing that left him clutching his chest and gasping for breath. A working life in the dusty air of the mill was telling on Jack Blake. Any emotional upheaval affected him thus.

'Want to be part of it! That's good, that is,' the miller wheezed, taking a handkerchief from his pocket and mopping his watering eyes. Recovering, he went on, 'Let me tell you this, my lad. You stand as much chance of going to sea as flying to the moon. What about my mill? Who's going to run it after I'm gone? This is a thriving concern. It takes more than one person to keep it going.'

'So? Father, you've got Cameron and Will, and the business is making enough to take on another man if need be. Surely one of us can be spared to follow our persuasion?'

'Follow your persuasion!' Miller Blake scowled. 'Have you any idea what you might be letting yourself in for? The sea's no picnic, y'know. 'Tis a dangerous environment to be sure.'

'And a mill isn't? What about Ed Moreton? Worked here man and boy and fell to his death working the pulleys — a task he'd done countless times before.'

'He was distracted. It only takes seconds, you know that.'

'Father, please.' Thomas's voice broke.

With rough sympathy his father rose quickly from his chair and went to grip his son by the shoulders.

'Forget it, boy. Put your mind to working here. It's a good living — better than rolling about on a ship day after blitherin' day, sick as a dog, not able to keep down a swallow of ale.'

'That's nothing!' Thomas shook his father off. 'A man gets used to it.'

Miller Blake's eyes narrowed cunningly. 'What about that little maid you've been walking out with? Sally, isn't it?'

'Sally Dimelow, yes. I've not kept anything from her. Sally knows my mind.'

'She won't like you going off and leaving her, never knowing when you'll be back — or if! I'm telling you straight, boy. A woman wants her man on the other side of the hearth of an evening, not the other side of the world.'

'Sally knows what's what. I've never pretended I'd be here for her day after day.'

'Then she's got less sense than I

credited her with.'

'Father, please . . . '

On and on went the voices. Hannah pegged the final shirt on the washing line, picked up the empty basket and left the orchard. Six weeks had gone by and she was coming to know the family; their strengths and weaknesses, their aspirations.

Cameron, betrothed to Lizzie Marsh from the Alport, was all set to make the mill his life's work, wanted nothing more. Hannah was aware of a growing fondness for Cameron, which she put down to gratitude at bringing her to the mill and restoring her self-esteem. Or was it more than that? At this point the sheer impossibility of the situation would overwhelm her and she would school her thoughts sternly to order.

Will, loveable tearaway Will, might have been the family's bane but all agreed that his saving grace was his astonishing affinity with horses. From the kitchen window Hannah had watched him bring round an ill-tempered beast, destined for the knacker's yard until Will had seen its potential and brought it home. Patiently, painstakingly, the lad had worked on the animal and now it stood every chance of making someone a worthy saddle horse.

For Jack Blake his youngest was clearly a source of worry, but on this occasion he had been full of praise for him.

After which Will had gone and spoiled it all with a night's carousing with his comrades and fallen into trouble with the Law, smashing a shop window in a drunken brawl.

He now sat at the kitchen table, nursing his wounds and his grievances. The situation had got out of hand and Will had not come off lightly. One look and Hannah had fetched warm salt water and a clean cloth.

'You spoil yourself, Will Blake!' she chastened him, dabbing gently at a cut lip. 'If you were my lad you'd get a good slap.'

'Go ahead.' Will sent her a lop-sided grin and held out a hand, which she slapped away in a mixture of frustration and uncontrolled laughter. It was impossible to be cross with Will for very long.

'Away with you! I'm serious. You're not doing yourself any favours by keeping in with that rough crowd. There are better things you could be about.'

'Like what?'

'Well, the horses. Will, you've magic in your hands there. What you're doing is a great skill and there will always be a demand for a reliable saddle animal. Tell me, how much do you charge when you sell one of the horses on?' she questioned.

'Charge? Oh, not a lot. Enough to put a guinea or two down on another nag, and maybe buy a few oats so Father doesn't grumble about me helping myself to the mill-horse's rations, and that's about it.'

'A guinea or two! Will, you could

double that. Treble it, even. Where's your business sense? You must have learned something from growing up here.'

A slow dawning crept over the lad's bruised face. 'Are you saying I should go into business with the 'osses? You're telling me I should buy in youngsters and train them up to sell, aren't you? It couldn't be done, Hannah. A man has to have the right set-up for that. I'd need a stableyard, grazing land, paddocks, something on the lines the Marquis of Cholmondeley has got, to make it pay properly. I could never rise to that. Besides, Father wouldn't hear of it. I'm destined for the mill like the others.'

'Do you like the work?' Hannah asked curiously.

'Oh, aye. I like it well enough. It's a living, isn't it? The 'osses are something different. I fit them in when I can.'

'Then who's to say you can't do both, but in a more organised way?'

Will thought on the suggestion,

frowning a little. 'Granted, you could have a point.'

'Think about it,' Hannah pressed. 'There's stabling here for an animal or two and if push came to shove you could rent more grazing land. There's always a farmer willing to tack out a few acres. You could run it as a sideline, a lucrative one. Build up a reputation for selling a reliable mount, and I wouldn't be a bit surprised if the work doesn't pour in. Then you can take stock and reconsider the situation.'

'Maybe.' He seemed torn, as if he wanted to believe in what she said but could not accept that it could happen . . . but then he was just a boy yet, Hannah told herself, with a boy's doubts and misgivings. He went on, more forcefully, 'I do like the 'osses, it's true. They're honest beasts. 'Tisn't them to blame when they go wrong, it's a result of bad handling. You've got to wipe all that out and get them to trust you. Once you've done that it's plain sailing — well, most of the time.

168

There's nothing like a good 'oss.' He glanced up at the clock on the wall. 'Lord save us, look at the time. Father'll go spare if he catches me lounging around here. Thanks for patching me up, Hannah.'

Will got up and left the premises, but his face had been serious and Hannah was hopeful that a seed had been sown.

As to Thomas's problem — well, he had her sympathy, she thought as she set about peeling the usual stack of potatoes for tonight's supper. She knew well enough what it was like to crave. As a girl she had cherished a secret yearning to run a small business of her own — a drapery shop, tearooms, anything. Being born female and without means had been a double drawback, putting paid to any hopes in that direction. On the other hand, she could empathise with Miller Blake. She had had a taste of the havoc the sea could wreak on a family, and it had left its mark. Though she also knew how strong the pull of the sea could be and her feelings swung back to Thomas and the dilemma he was in.

Hannah tipped the vegetables into the pot, added salt and a sprinkling of herbs and swung the vessel over the fire. She was deliberating between a milk pudding and a jam pasty for afterwards when the door burst open and Thomas stalked in.

'I've had enough!' he said bitterly. 'I want to get out. You were there, Hannah. You must have heard what went on.'

'I couldn't help but overhear some of it. Thomas, your father is only thinking of your own good.'

'He's thinking of the mill. That's all that matters to him. I'm not like Father. I've got other aspirations.'

'I know, and it's hard for you. What does your girl say about it?' she asked.

'Me going for a sailor?' He pulled a face. 'Sally's as bad as Father if the truth be known. We're not promised. She's free to find someone else if she wants.'

'Is that what you want?'

Thomas shrugged. 'No, it isn't. Sally's the light of my life. I'd never find another like her. I don't know. Other girls get wed to seafarers and don't make any bones about it. Why can't she? Why doesn't she stop the arguments?'

'Maybe she thinks she can twist you round her little finger.'

A smile touched his lips. 'Well, she can most of the time.'

'Though not in this case, it seems. Would you like me to put in a word?'

'You'd speak to Father?' he said eagerly.

'I would if the opportunity presented itself, though I'd need to have a care. I am an employee here, remember. I have to mind my place.'

'Father wouldn't mind. He thinks too highly of you. Still, I wouldn't want to be the cause of trouble. Hannah, if you could speak to Sally I'd appreciate it. Make her see that being a sailor's wife isn't all bad. She's too close to me to take it. Happen she'll listen to you. I hope so, anyway. Anything's worth a try. Will you try?'

'I'll do my best,' Hannah said.

★ ★ ★

'Sally, try and look at it this way,' Hannah began, having met the girl on the heath when she was on her way to Brook Cottage. 'It's true that Thomas would be away for weeks on end and I can see how upsetting that appears, especially for a young bride. But just think, he'd be home for long spells too. You'd have him all to yourself. Imagine how marvellous that would be.'

'Yes, there is that.' Sally still looked doubtful.

The evening was warm and balmy and filled with the scent of drying grass. In the fields the men were turning the hay and their voices carried over the air.

'Every time his ship came in there would be that special reunion. Why, you'd remain sweethearts all your lives.

He'd bring you gifts, rarities from foreign parts. You would be the envy of your neighbours.' Hannah smiled.

'Yes. I suppose you're right. We've got a ginger jar at home that came from China. It's my ma's greatest treasure. I don't know who she got it from but it's real pretty. Do you think it's right, what you said about remaining sweethearts?'

'I'm sure of it. How could it be otherwise? He'd be searching the line of wives and children and sweethearts at the quayside from the deck of his ship. It would be your face that would stand out for him. There could be a new babe in your arms, God willing. What a prize to be able to show him. All your own work, too — well, almost.'

Sally giggled, blushing. She was looking a great deal more positive and Hannah pressed her advantage home. 'You would never fall into the trap of so many married couples and grow weary of each other's company. It happens, you know. Not with everyone, but there's always the danger of taking each other for granted, don't you agree?'

'Well, yes . . . but a seaman leads a perilous life,' Sally blurted out. 'Imagine how worried I'd always be, thinking of him being lost in a storm or set upon by ruffians in some faraway land and robbed, or hurt — or worse.'

'Oh, Sally. I allow there's danger.' Hannah thought of her father and pushed the memory aside. 'But there is danger everywhere. And Thomas would not be alone. He would have the company and support of his fellow men.'

'Yes, but how would you feel if it were you, wondering if every time you kissed your man goodbye it was the last time?' Sally clapped her hand across her mouth. 'Oh, forget I said that. 'Twas thoughtless of me, you being a widow and all.'

'It's all right.' Hannah felt the usual stab of guilt and took a calming breath. 'I know what you mean and I confess it would not be easy. But think on. You'll have those children, babies to look after and cherish. Children fill your days and help take your mind off brooding. You would have a home to care for, too. Think of it — your own little home to furnish exactly as you please.'

Sally nodded, dimpled face serious. A pretty girl, her clear green eyes and flaxen hair was a perfect foil to Thomas's robust darkness. In her gown of sprigged cotton with a sash of green, matching ribbons in her bonnet, she looked trim and fresh. Hannah could see how Thomas was so taken with her.

'Maybe I've been hasty,' Sally said at last. 'Mother told me I shouldn't have said what I did. She said there's nothing more likely to frighten a suitor off than a nag. Would you say I've put Thomas off, ma'am?'

'Not for one moment. And please do call me Hannah. Ma'am makes me feel like an old biddy with bitterness on her lips.'

'You'd never be that. I'd be pleased to call you by name. It means we're friends.'

'Yes, it does, doesn't it?'

Sally cast a glance towards the fork in the path where Thomas would be waiting for her. 'Hannah, I'd best go. Thomas will be wondering where I am.'

'Me, too. Vinnie and Madge will be looking out for me, bless them. Don't forget, there are worse things than being wed to a seafarer, Sally.'

'I won't.' Sally sent a nod and went on her way and Hannah continued along the leafy path to Cuddington.

Madge was waiting for her at the gate with Vinnie in her arms.

'Mama!' the child said, holding out her arms. 'Mama!'

'Oh, you're talking! You said Mama.' Hannah took her up and twirled her round. 'Clever girl!'

'I've been trying for days to get her to say it and she came out with it this morning,' Madge said. 'With no prompting, either. She's forward for her age, Hannah.'

'Do you think so?' Hannah couldn't keep the smile from her face. 'Clever

Vinnie! Mama's clever girl! Oh, I do love you!'

'She had a ride on the trap pony today. Insisted upon it, no less. She's no fear at all, and Nobby was as quiet as could be with her. Proper little farmer's lass, she is.'

'Would that it were really so, Madge,' Hannah said, her eyes looking inwards.

Madge cast her a curious glance. 'There now. You've gone all downcast. Cheer up. Kettle's boiled. Let's have a cup of tea.'

'That would be lovely. I must not be too long. I met Sally Dimelow on the way here and we got talking. It's made me late.'

Over the tea — a fresh straining, Hannah noticed, and not the carefully hoarded leaves of several brews as before — she told Madge about Thomas's problem.

Madge heaved a sigh. 'Miller Blake's a good man but he's wrong to hold Thomas back from the sea. If he's not careful the lad will up and leave of his own volition and that'll be that. They'll be lucky if they ever see him again. Far better to bend with the wind, I'm thinking.'

'I'm sure you are right.' Hannah took a bite of freshly-baked gingerbread, savouring the flavour. 'Mmm, this is good.'

'I'll let you have the recipe. 'Tis one passed down through the family and you're as near to a daughter as I'll have.'

It was not the first time this had been said and Hannah blushed with pleasure. *If only it were truly so*, she thought. Friendship was one thing and blood ties another, and everyone knew which was the stronger.

'That Sally Dimelow is a sweet maid,' Madge went on, stirring her tea. 'She's a different kettle of fish to the other one. Cameron's girl, you know.'

'Lizzie?' Hannah raised her eyes heavenwards. 'She doesn't care for me. Goodness knows why. I've never done anything to rile her. At least, I don't think so.'

'It's likely just her way.'

'I make sure and keep my place when she's there. She delights in putting me in the wrong and showing me up in front of the others.'

'Ah well, I daresay she won't take kindly to you and her betrothed biding under the same roof.'

'But that is so silly.'

'Of course it is, and Lizzie Marsh probably knows it deep down. That won't stop her tantrums, though. She's a waspish creature and no mistake. Her ma and pa have spoilt her. Whatever she wanted was hers. It doesn't do to spoil your children. They grow up into spoilt adults, and that's no good to them nor the folks around them.'

'I shall remember that with Vinnie.'

'Oh, I think you've got it just right. If you ask me, that Lizzie would be more suited to a life of being pampered and petted than wife to a hard-working miller. She's got a good brain, mind. Writes poetry, I'm told. Still, making pretty verse isn't the be-all and end-all, is it? I'm thinking Cameron will have to take a firm hand with her or he'll end up being hen-pecked.' Madge picked up the teapot. 'More tea?'

'No, I had better not, thank you.' Hannah stood up. 'I should really be going, Madge, but I shall put Vinnie to bed first. Come along, my pet. My, what a big girl you are growing into. You get heavier every time I lift you up, my darling,' she said, kissing the top of her silky head.

It was hard tearing herself away. After singing her child to sleep she snatched a few more moments to stand and gaze at the little girl's chubby face. Hannah wished it had been her own ears that had heard the first word pass those lips — but there, she admonished herself, things could be worse. Pressing a kiss on Vinnie's forehead, she tiptoed out of the room and hurried down the stairs to say goodbye to Madge.

Shadows were long-drawn across the path as she sped back to the mill to prepare supper.

On the forecourt, Cameron was talking to Lizzie. Seeing Hannah, the girl's face sharpened.

'There you are, Hannah,' Cameron greeted. 'It's getting dark. You shouldn't be out on your own.'

'Oh, really, Cameron,' Lizzie said, scowling, her not unattractive face losing its charm. She tossed back a ringlet of light-brown hair. 'Hannah's used to her own company. It is how servants have to be.'

'Maybe, but it's a lonely step and you never know who's around,' Cameron said. 'Hannah, once the days start drawing in, it might be best if one of us comes to meet you.'

'Oh, no, really. I can always take a lantern. It is my choice to go so frequently to Madge's and I would not want to be any trouble to anyone.'

'Who said anything about trouble? It would be a pleasure and I'm sure Father would see the sense in it.'

During the conversation Lizzie's scowl deepened. She looked about to put in a word of protest, but at that moment the rattle of iron wheels and clopping of hooves sounded on the lane and her father drove onto the forecourt in his high-sprung black-painted trap.

'Evening, Cameron. Ma'am.' He raised his cap to Hannah, drawing yet another frown from his daughter. 'Hop in then, our Lizzie. Look sharp, I've a cow calving. I want to get back to her.'

Without a word to her betrothed Lizzie flounced into the trap, and as they drove away her voice could be heard, loudly berating her father for addressing a servant in so genteel a manner. Mortified colour touched Hannah's cheekbones. She gathered up her skirts and hurried towards the millhouse. Cameron, however, was quick to catch up with her.

'You mustn't heed Lizzie,' he said, striding ahead to open the door for her. 'She doesn't mean anything by it.'

'No, I am sure. Perhaps it is I who am remiss. I sometimes pass a few words with her papa when I see him. It was Farmer Marsh who let us have the cat, and he always makes a point of asking if she is still doing the job she was got for. It might be wiser to hold back.'

'Nonsense. You've as much right to a conversation with a neighbour as the next person. It's commendable the way you've fitted in here. Even the customers have started enquiring after you and that's something.'

He went for a change of subject. 'You'll have been visiting that little maid of yours. How did you find her?'

'Oh, growing up fast.' Relieved that the awkward moment was passed, Hannah told him about her child's newfound speech. 'It has just been baby talk until now but today she called me 'mama' quite distinctly. I'm so proud of her.'

'Aye, you must be. It's tragic for you, having no one to share these moments with. What a good thing you've got the Widow — and us, of course. I know what Father said about a mill being no place for an infant, but 'twould be nice for you to have your little'n here with you. Happen in the fullness of time he'll come round, though.'

Cameron smiled down at her, a smile that went right to the depths of his striking blue eyes, and Hannah's heart gave another of those curious little bumps. It was a feeling she had never before experienced and she was glad of the dimness of the narrow hallway that hid the glow that rushed to her cheeks for a second time.

'Yes, well. We shall have to wait and see,' she said breathlessly. 'Pray excuse me, Cameron. I'll just take off my bonnet and shawl and then I'll get the supper. I'm running late. Your father will be over from the mill if I'm not careful, and no food on the table.'

She slipped past him and went running up the stair. By the time she entered her room her heart was thumping all the more — but was it from her wild flight, or something more?

10

During one cloud-swept morning in August, rain spattering against the window pane, Hannah decided to tackle the attic — a task she had been putting off.

Used for decades as a general store, it was stacked with unwanted pieces of furniture, heavy iron-bound wooden chests full of old curtains, drapes and bedcovers that had seen better days, and sundry other household items that had long outlived their usefulness.

Swathed from head to foot in a voluminous pinafore that must have belonged to a previous housekeeper, her hair bundled into a frilled cap against the dust and the cobwebs, Hannah set to work dragging everything moveable to one side.

One of the chests was heavier than the rest. Peering inside to find out why this should be, she found it crammed with old office ledgers, the leather binding dry and cracked, figuring faded and illegible. Resting on the top was a smaller book. Curious, Hannah opened it.

'Sarah Jane Blake. Her Journal. Eighteen Hundred and Nine,' she read aloud.

The writing, in flowing script, was also faded in places but the work was still reasonably easy to read. Hannah assumed that the scriber was grandmother to the Blake boys and leafed through the pages, noting a great many blank ones. She was about to return it to the chest when she thought again. The moving of the bigger items in the attic had been no easy task and she was ready to rest her aching muscles for a moment or two, so closing the lid of the chest she sat to read some more.

★   ★   ★

Thursday, January 1st.
We have had heavy frost and I did

not expect callers, so I was overjoyed to see my good friend Hannah Mary pulling up outside in the dog-cart. She had been shopping to Malpas and called on her way home to Agden. Little Alice was with her, all bundled up in shawls against the cold. Bless the child, her cheeks were pink and her eyes bright.

I gave Hannah Mary much praise for the way in which she is looking after her small niece. Alice was barely toddling when her mama passed on and it cannot have been easy for a spinster of Hannah Mary's years to give up a quiet life of study and reflection and take on so young an infant.

★   ★   ★

Hannah's heart pounded. Hannah Mary? Alice? This was far too near the mark to be brushed off as coincidence! Alice, her mother's name. If what her mind was telling her was true, it followed that Sarah Jane Blake's friend was none other than her namesake, the great-aunt who had brought her mother up. She thought of the dreams that felt so real. Yet there were discrepancies here. Leaving it for the moment, she read on.

A few pages onwards she saw a reference to a dear brother, Bertie, sailing the southern seas, no word of him for months and what a worry it was for the family.

Bertie! This evidently was the seafaring relative that had inspired Thomas Blake to want to follow in his footsteps. Hannah's mind went back to the baffling aspect in the dreams and she screwed up her face, trying to make some sort of sense of the name the child called her aunt. *Auntannie*. It was a peculiar term of address but then the child was very young, maybe not yet in her fourth year and she spoke in an excited babble that at times the two women found difficult to follow. The name Annie for the woman had been the obvious assumption but now

Hannah thought again. Almost of its own volition, her gaze strayed to one of the names on the written page — it was her own name, Hannah.

Of course! Realisation struck her with suddenness that brought a choking cry from her throat and she could have shaken herself for not having worked it out before. Hannie! It was Hannie the child was trying to say and not Annie as she had thought. Aunt Hannie must have been her baby name for her aunt Hannah Mary. That settled the matter. There was no other explanation, and the implications of it all just about took Hannah's breath away. The small girl she was seeing in those strange pictures that the Parkgate wise woman had called waking dreams was her very own mother; her mother as a lively child with the aunt who had been her guardian and mentor — Hannah Mary Carraway.

Hannah's heart thudded and the room began to spin about her with the shock of the discovery. Taking several sustaining breaths, she waited for the world to stop rocking and reeling and went back to the journal. Most of the writing involved small day-to-day events; a delivery of grain overturning on the road, the husband's annoyance at customers who failed to pay their bills on time — an event common enough today and equally as infuriating to the tradesman in question. Another gasp escaped her lips at a second reference to the friend from Agden.

⋆ ⋆ ⋆

Wednesday, May 20th

I have been poorly and was greatly cheered by a visit from Hannah Mary. She had left Alice with Madge Nightingale, playing with a litter of kittens — a wise move, the sickroom is no place for a child.

How sad that Jane died. She was such a gentle creature and a good mother to little Alice. That scoundrel of a husband deserves a thrashing for the way he treated her and for his recent behaviour.

How could he go off and forsake his little daughter in this uncouth way?

It does not bear thinking about.

★   ★   ★

Poor Mother, Hannah thought sorrowfully, feeling the sting of tears. *What a tragic start to a small life.* She wondered why her mother had never talked of it. All she had ever spoken of was Hannah Mary's fortitude at raising her when really she had been wedded to a quiet, spinsterish existence with her books.

Hannah had no idea what had become of her namesake after her mother had married and moved with her young husband to Parkgate. Perhaps the woman was dead by this time, but if so, why was she not buried here in St Oswald's churchyard?

A horse and cart rumbling into the forecourt below had Hannah darting to the window to see who it was. Cameron was back from delivering a load of millings. Soon the others would be in for their midday meal. Time had run away with her. She had better leave off what she was doing and go downstairs and check the midday broth. Her mind still reeling from her discovery, she slipped the journal into her pocket to read more thoroughly when she had a spare moment.

★   ★   ★

'Agden?' Cameron regarded her with surprise. Of all the Blakes, Cameron was proving the most approachable if she needed to know anything or wanted assistance with a situation she could not manage by herself. He had come in ahead of the rest of the family and, with the journal burning a reminder in her pocket, Hannah had seized her chance to quiz him over its contents. 'Why, 'tis on the road to Grindley Brook, roughly an hour's drive from here. Why do you want to know?'

'Oh, I just happened to hear about it and wondered,' Hannah said, reluctant to admit too much at this point. 'What sort of place would it be? Is it a village like Cuddington?'

'Well, you could say that. It's more spread out, perhaps, nothing remarkable, just a scattering of cottages, farms, a couple of shops . . . the usual. There's a good smith at Agden. Will uses him for his horses, says he'd trust no other. The fellow's rates are reasonable, too, he doesn't charge as much as Hampton or Malpas.'

He went to the washstand under the window where Hannah had placed warm water, yellow soap and a cloth, and with a great deal of splashing he washed the flour-dust from his hands and forearms, shaking the water from his hands before drying himself off with the cloth. After this ritual he came to sit at the table which Hannah was setting for the midday meal; a standard repast of good thick vegetable broth, new-made bread and generous wedges of cheese, washed down with strong sweet tea or ale.

'Does Agden have a church?' Hannah went on hopefully, dipping into a drawer for the cutlery, placing bread on the table. The find in the attic had re-sparked the desire to trace her family in full force and a churchyard seemed an ideal place to start.

'Aye, a small one. There's a chapel as well as the church. That's fairly new, of course. I remember it going up. There was a fuss about it being built where it was. Nobody could agree on whose land it belonged to.' Cameron ran his hand over his unruly mop of hair in thought, making it more untidy than ever. 'Tell you what. I shall be going that way later in the week. There's a keg of cider to pick up from the Horse and Jockey and I promised the fellow at the farm next to it I'd call for his few bags of grains that need milling. Well, he's getting on in years, doesn't want to be mauling heavy sacks around. It'll be Thursday or Friday, I can't say which at this point. Why don't you come with me?'

Hannah's better self told her this could be a dangerous move, but the offer was too much to resist.

'Oh, could I? Or perhaps I shouldn't. It's a working day, after all. I'd best ask your father first.'

'Father won't mind. Why should he? We'd not be away all that long. Thinking about it, there's a handy village store at Agden. Mother used to take Thomas and me there in the trap to spend our pennies. We'd buy liquorice sticks and barley sugar twists and the wife would give us an extra measure if we promised to be good. As far as I recall, it was a well-stocked little place. It'd give you the chance to pick up some supplies, and save us a trip to Malpas — that town is getting busier with every day that passes. If you can find a speck for the horse and cart on the High Street you consider yourself fortunate. I'll tell Father, if you like.'

'Oh, splendid!' Hannah wanted to clap her hands together in glee. 'There is always something I am short of for the larder. I know for a fact we're getting low on potatoes and carrots. I never do seem to buy enough. I had better make a list.'

'There you are, then.' Cameron sent her a beaming smile that made her heart constrict painfully. 'I'll be going early, mind. What if I drop you off at the store and pick you up on the way back? How does that suit?'

'Perfect,' Hannah answered, setting the table with more clatter than was necessary.

★ ★ ★

For reasons she did not go into too deeply, she made a special effort with her appearance for the trip. She put on her gown of blue kerseymere — the one she had worn for the office at the salt mine; it seemed a lifetime ago — and her best bonnet, tweaking a few glossy brown-black curls becomingly onto her forehead. Studying herself in the looking glass on the parlour wall, she decided a little adornment was necessary and from under her chemise she pulled out the locket she still wore at her neck, a bitter-sweet reminder of her mother. It looked very fine against the kerseymere and giving herself a satisfied little nod, she brushed an imagined crease from her skirts and quickly left the room.

There was no mistaking the admiration in Cameron's eyes as she emerged from the house, two deep wicker baskets in her hands, the shopping list tucked into her purse.

Miller Blake had told her to make free with the household cash, kept in a small wooden coffer on the dresser, and the purse was agreeably heavy, stowed away in the deep pocket of her skirts.

'Well now, aren't we grand? I reckon we should be taking the horse and trap and not this old working cart,' Cameron said as he took the shopping baskets from her and placed them on the bed of the vehicle, before helping her onto the front where he had arranged a wad of clean hessian sacks for her to sit on. 'Reckon I'll be the envy of the village. It's not every day I have a bonny young lass up beside me.'

'Go on with you! I'm no young lass. I'm an old married woman with a child, as well you know. So let's have less of the flattery, Cameron Blake!' A smile belied her words, though. Hannah was secretly pleased at the attention received from her smiling companion.

Cameron shot her a glance. 'I stand to correct you there, Hannah. You're an attractive young widow. Why some fellow hasn't snapped you up before now, I'll never know. The menfolk hereabouts must be blind.'

The reference to her supposed widowhood brought the expected rush of guilt, and Hannah was glad when Cameron sprang aboard the cart and whipped up the horse with nothing more said.

They rumbled out of the yard and onto the lane, and she experienced a sharp sense of gratitude and relief when instead of taking the way that went past Alport Farm and risking the chance of being observed, which could have created a problem for her, Cameron without a word pulled off onto the Cuddington track that would also pick up the Welsh road and thence the highway to Agden and Grindley Brook.

There was no underhandedness in the action. It simply seemed a sensible precaution on his part, the sort of move that persons blessed with Cameron Blake's foresight were capable of, and yet Hannah was saddened that it was necessary.

She was adamant that Cameron's betrothed had nothing to fear from her, that it was perfectly in order for her to go with him to attend to the household shopping at a different source from the usual, and yet a small voice within told her that in this case a saying, 'What the eye does not see, the heart cannot grieve over' was more than appropriate.

Once they had gone past Brook Cottage — no sign of Madge and Vinnie, but then it was market day and they would probably have set out early for Hampton — Hannah settled down to enjoy the ride.

'How's Widow Nightingale managing without you there to give a hand?' Cameron asked with a backward glance at the cottage's neat acres. 'It can't be easy for her. She's no spring chicken, is she?'

'I know. It worries me. Sometimes she looks worn out and having Vinnie under her feet all day doesn't help matters. She's such a lively child.'

'That'll get easier when she's a mite older. Happen we could do something to help with the heavy work, though. Our Will could go over there and do a bit of digging and maybe chop her some firewood, if you like.'

'Do you think he'd mind?'

'It's what neighbours do, and the sooner he learns that, the better!' Cameron replied a little too sharply.

Hannah looked at him swiftly. 'You sound out of sorts with him. What's the matter? Has Will been up to his tricks again?'

'He was out with the crowd last night — troublemaking lot! Didn't you hear him come in?'

'No, but then I would not. Being in the back of the house, any sound is drowned out by the millrace.'

'Aye, it will be. I'd not thought of that. Does it disturb you?'

'Not in the least. I like to lie there and listen to the water. It sends me off to sleep.'

'That's all right, then,' Cameron said comfortably. 'Getting back to our Will, it was pretty late when he got in. The clock had long struck midnight. I had the devil's own job to rouse him this morning. Silly young fool.'

'He's just a boy. He'll see sense in time.'

'Think so? Seems to me it would be no bad thing if he concentrated more on his horses and less on trying to impress his fellows. When he's got a new animal to work on, these wild escapades of his are fewer. It gives him something else to think about, you see.'

'It works off a lot of surplus energy, too. I once suggested he took his skills a stage further and made the horses a second occupation.' She shot Cameron a wary glance. 'But there, perhaps I was speaking out of turn.'

'Get away. Of course you weren't. You were trying to knock some sense into him and that's no easy matter with our Will. You never know, what you said might have done some good. He's more likely to take notice of you than any of us. Let's hope so, anyway.' The road was uneven and the cart gave a sudden lurch, making Hannah grab hold of the side to keep her balance. 'Sorry about that,' Cameron apologised.

'It's quite all right. You need not

worry about me. i am accustomed to riding this way.'

'Maybe, but this is a fair bit further than nipping into town. A working cart isn't exactly the most comfortable mode of travel and old Captain's not one for stepping out.'

'Well, I am not complaining. What a lovely morning it is. So fresh and sweet after the rain.'

Hannah glanced about her. The wet spell had given way to bright sunshine. It was a pleasure to be trundling along, the sun warm on her face and the scent of rain-soaked ground ripe on the morning air.

'What's the sudden interest in Agden?' Cameron asked next. 'Do you have some acquaintance there?'

'I . . . well, there could be. I am not actually sure.'

'You sound guarded. I don't know, Hannah, you always do when anything personal crops up. What is it? I'm not one to intrude. I was just interested, that's all.'

He looked at her with a faintly injured air and she reached out and pressed his arm. 'I am sorry. I know I can be touchy at times. These past months have not been easy for me. When I first came here, people were not exactly hospitable. For a reason I cannot go into, I was not wearing my wedding ring — you can guess the rest.'

'Aye, well. You see many a woman with no wedding band on her finger. It doesn't necessarily mean anything. It's up to them . . . or else it's a result of what life has dealt them. Life's not easy for you womenfolk, I'm thinking.' He gave the reins a flip and the horse increased its plodding pace a fraction. 'Has the situation improved since?'

'In the main, yes, it has. I can hold my head up now when I go into town. You cannot imagine how good that feels.'

'I reckon I've an idea. Still, that's a step in the right direction. My guess is it's just the odd few tattle-tongues stirring things up for you, right?'

'Well, yes. Being housekeeper at the mill has helped the situation a great deal. Your father is very much respected in the community, is he not? I noticed a considerable difference in attitude after I came to work for you.'

'It takes a while for anybody to settle in a new area. Folks are wary of strangers, goodness knows why. You learn to take people as you find them, don't you? Didn't lodging with the Widow help things along? She's highly thought of and all.'

'Oh yes, but it took a while, though. I had to brace myself to go into town to do the Brook Cottage shopping.'

'Huh, that's good, that is!' Cameron said dourly, sounding so much like his sire that Hannah had to hide a smile. He went on, 'Some people like to make things hard for others, that's all I can say. Hannah, forgive me if I sound as if I'm prying, but can you name the person or persons you're looking for at Agden? You never know, I may be able to help.'

'Well . . . I . . . ' Hannah hesitated, and then without going into too much detail she told Cameron what she had discovered in the attic.

'An old journal? Really? Well, I never! Sarah Jane was our grandmother,' he replied.

'Yes, so I thought. I couldn't resist looking at it. There's something fascinating about a journal. It takes you right to the heart of a person's life, their thoughts and expectations. There isn't a lot in this one. Sarah Jane stopped writing in it in the September, though.'

'That would be when she was taken badly. She had a fever of the lungs, poor lady. She didn't last out the year. Is this what's sparked off the interest in Agden?'

'Yes. There's mention of a friend who visited. Her name was the same as mine. I know it's a commonplace enough name, only she was Hannah Mary and that narrowed things down a little. There was a Hannah Mary in my family, you see. In the journal she had a small charge with her, which turned out to be her niece. Would you know who they were?'

At that moment there was the sound of another vehicle on the road and a chaise bowled up quickly behind them. Throwing a glance over his shoulder, Cameron cursed quietly under his breath. 'Devil take it, they always appear where the way is narrowest! No patience, either. Always have to get past, as if they need to be wherever they're heading in two minutes flat!'

Hannah tried to curb her impatience as he manoeuvred the horse and unwieldy cart into the side for the other driver to pass.

'A woman and her niece, you say?' he said once they had set off again. 'I can't help you there. You're best asking Father — or Widow Nightingale. She'd know folks that lived hereabouts around that time.'

'Yes, it's true. They came from Agden,' Hannah persisted. 'I thought I'd take a look around the churchyard.'

'It's as good a start as any, though you'll not find Sarah Jane there. She was laid to rest at St Oswald's, same as all the Blakes before her.' Cameron clicked his tongue to the horse.

'Get up there, Captain!'

★ ★ ★

Alighting at Agden outside the village store, Hannah watched the cart go lumbering off before going into the shop to make her purchases. When she mentioned that she would like to look around the village, the shopkeeper obligingly offered to look after her shopping for her.

'That's very kind. I do not expect to be too long.'

She sent him a smile and left, shop-bell clanging after her, and soon afterwards she was letting herself in through the lych-gate of the small country church with its arched windows and square tower.

Spreading yews gave a deep shade

and ranks of leaning and mossy headstones told of decades of quiet rest. There was the busy hum of insects, a scent of grass and flowers that had sown themselves over the centuries; blue periwinkle, red herb Robert and some pretty starred white blooms that Hannah could not name. Lifting her skirts, for the grass was still wet from recent downpours, she began a methodical search of the graves, starting by the boundary wall.

Not for the first time, she berated herself for not having been more attentive when her mother had spoken of her family — when she had mentioned them at all, that was. Surely, Hannah asked herself, her mother must have told her the given names of her grandparents at some point? For the life of her she could not muster any recollection of it. Confusing the issue further was the fact that many of the mounds here had no stones to mark who lay underneath the turf.

She was about to give up when,

11

'Miss Carraway! Good morning to you, ma'am. I'm pleased to see you.' The clergyman briefly takes the woman's thin hand in greeting. 'May I enquire after your young charge? She is well and thriving, I hope?'

'Very much so, thank you, Rector.'

Warming sunlight slants in through the open doorway of the church porch. Members of the congregation gather in chattering groups on the steps and pathways outside. Behind the woman, yet more worshippers have yet to leave the mellow confines of the church building.

'Excellent, excellent.' The clergyman smiles and presses a pamphlet into her hands.

She takes it, looking confused.

'Just a token of how we at St Asaph's look after our church. Please don't distress yourself unduly, ma'am. It's but a list of church duties. The kind ladies of the parish like to keep the building pristine and make sure there are fresh flowers on the altar — when it is appropriate to the church calendar, naturally,' he explains.

'I see. My thanks. I shall acquaint myself with it at some point,' she replies.

'Yes, do, dear lady. Well then, it is to be hoped we see your ward at the Sunday School before long? My good lady was saying only this morning how thin on the ground the classes are. The village is sadly diminished since we first came here, I'm sorry to say. The sickness last winter carried a dearth of people off. It's a sad fact but the elderly and the young are always the most vulnerable.'

'Indeed you are right. Rector, I feel I should point out that my niece is but a baby as yet. I wouldn't want to overwhelm her with too much learning too soon. And she has had to cope with much in her short life.'

'Quite, quite. You are comfortable at your change of abode, Miss Carraway?'

'Yes, it is more than adequate, thank you,' she replies.

'Anything we can do, you have only to ask. Mary — my good wife — keeps a store of children's clothing; used, you understand, but quite serviceable. Should you require anything just ask and — '

'Thank you, Rector, it is generous of you in the extreme but keeping one small person in garments is not beyond my means or my capabilities. Now, if you'll please excuse me. I have left my niece with a kindly neighbour. I am sure she will be wondering where I am . . .'

* * *

'Change of abode,' Hannah murmured, sleepily batting at a pestering fly with her hand.

Her face was hot and scorched with the sun and she thought about moving

214

to the shade, but she was on the whole too comfortable where she was.

★ ★ ★

The figures fade, the voices ebb away and the scene changes. The aunt sits reading a letter in the window embrasure of a small, dim, wood-panelled parlour that has one wall lined floor to celling with books.

Rustling issues from the wainscot and she glances up.

'Mice again,' *she complains.* 'I must see about getting a cat or we shall be overrun.'

She returns to her letter, frowning, her hand going to her brow in a gesture of dismay.

'So he has wed the doxy he took up with! 'Tis no different to what I expected, and yet one hoped that his better self would have nudged him into first considering his child. Poor little waif. No mama, and my sister was such a vibrant, laughing creature; only this* *dour, spinsterish creature left for her to relate to. Ah me, I cannot help feeling that a child needs both parents. A father's influence goes a long way to helping a young person to adjust to the world. And nobody is all bad, I suppose. Roger had a winning side to his nature; how else could my dearest sister have fallen under his spell?'*

★　★　★

'Hannah! Hannah, wake up. It's all right. You're quite safe.'

Hannah's eyes blinked open. *A father's influence goes a long way towards helping a child to adjust to the world.* The words echoed in her mind; strident, accusing.

'What have I done?' she cried out in confusion. The sun was in her eyes and she could not make out the face that loomed over her. 'Help me. Oh, please, help me right the wrong!'

'Hannah. Listen to me. It's me, Cameron. You're all right, my dear.

216

Come along. Try and sit up.'

Strong, gentle hands supported her. She was sobbing wildly, tears coursing down her sun-scorched cheeks. Her carefully arranged hair had escaped its pins and tumbled in a profusion of curls and waves almost to her waist. She felt a hand stroke it wonderingly, and then Cameron sat down beside her, drew her to him and let her sob, enfolded in his arms.

Gradually the weeping subsided, even though the cause of the outburst did not. *Vinnie*, she thought, her mind fevered and racing. Had she been over-hasty and done her child a mis-service by removing her from her father? Was this history repeating itself? Would Edward have come round, in time, to accepting another female child, as the stern-faced aunt in the dream had hoped of the man who had deserted her sister and the baby?

Hannah was at a loss to find an answer.

Cameron withdrew his arms. 'Are

you feeling better?'

'What? Why, yes. No. Oh, I do not know.' She felt utterly foolish. 'I am so sorry. I sat down to wait for you. I was tired and must have dozed.'

'It's unwise to fall asleep in the sun. Your nose is quite pink. The skin will peel if you're not careful.'

He was smiling, trying to put her at her ease, but his eyes brimmed with curiosity and a gentle sympathy.

Hannah's hands flew to her face, feeling its heat that was not only due to the beating rays of the sun. 'I . . . I was dreaming. I often dream. It is nothing. Take no notice. I shall be all right in a moment or two.'

''Course you will,' Cameron answered and, bending, he pressed a kiss on her forehead. Brief though it was, brotherly and lacking in passion, the fire that shot through Hannah's blood was every bit as scorching as the sun was.

'Hannah, I feel you are troubled. It's said a trouble shared is a trouble halved, though I don't know how true that is. If ever you need a listening ear, you know where to come, don't you?'

'I . . . yes. Thank you.'

'Don't thank me, I've done nothing. Here.' He picked up her discarded bonnet. 'Put this on, it'll protect your head on the way back. Can't have you being poorly with heatstroke, can we? Who'd get our meals on the table if you were out of action? Cart's loaded and ready for off.'

'That was quick.'

'Oh, I've been here a while. Had to leave the horse and cart in a side street; there was no room outside the stores. You were bent over a tombstone when I glanced this way so I reckoned I'd best leave you to it for a bit. Did you have any luck?'

Hannah shook her head, which was beginning to ache dully. She didn't want to think about what had happened or what had provoked it. The imprint of Cameron's kiss burned on her skin and his kindness, far from being balm to her troubled soul, only caused her to shrivel inside with guilt and remorse.

She felt a fraud, living this life under such a kindly roof as the Blakes'. She had not directly lied but misled, and she was not proud of it. Madge Nightingale's trusting face floated into her mind and guilt pierced her afresh.

'Come on,' Cameron said, pulling to his feet and holding out his hands to help her. 'Let's go and find the cart. You can tidy yourself up on the drive back. Won't do to turn up at the house looking as if you've been dragged through a hedge backwards, will it?' he said, smiling.

'Not really,' she managed to choke.

Hannah was quiet on the journey back. Cameron too had little to say and they sat side by side on the cart, each lost in their own thoughts, while the horse put on a little spurt, eager for his stable and the feed that was waiting.

★ ★ ★

Cameron, stacking sacks of wheat in the grain-loft that evening, was mystified. What had upset Hannah so? She had been cheery as a sparrow when they had set out, looking a treat in her blue gown and pretty bonnet. His mind roamed on, puzzled in the extreme. Why the interest in a place as nondescript as Agden, for pity's sake? She'd been crouching at one of the older graves in the churchyard as if her attention was riveted on it. He wondered who was interred there, and if the discovery had been responsible for her bad dreams. She had been reluctant to talk about it — but then that was Hannah, close as a clam in some respects, an open book in others.

How lovely she was, he thought, not for the first time. That kiss; the melting quality in those drenched dark eyes when she had looked up at him. He shouldn't have kissed her but at the time it had seemed the natural thing to do, a token of comfort. How he wished she could be his.

Cameron heaved the final sack onto the platform and worked the pulleys that would transport the load to the ground floor. Lately he was beset by the feeling that he had made a terrible mistake about the future, but what was done was done. It was too late to go back.

Disturbed by the loud clanking and creaking of the iron chains of the pulley system, a rat ran across the main rafter overhead, reared up on its haunches and chattered angrily at him. Cameron picked up a brick kept handy to balance an uneven load and flung it with all his strength. It missed and the creature scuttled off and with a whisk of its long tail, vanished into the wall. The thump of the falling brick reverberated emptily through the building and quickly faded away.

12

'Come, my child, come with me. Let me show you how to make a tossy-ball.'

'What's that, Auntannie?'

'Child, how many times do I have to remind you not to drop your h's? Say 'hah'.'

'ah. Is that better? The tossy-ball, Auntannie. Wemember?'

'As if I'd be allowed to forget! It's a ball made of cowslips. See them, down there by the brook, those pretty yellow flowers? Shall we go and pick some?'

'Oh yes! Watch me wun. I can wun fast!'

The child sprints off, bonnet strings flying, voice carrying on the breeze.

'Careful, Alice. Mind the water. It runs deep just there.'

The woman quickens her step to catch up with the fleeing child, and both arrived breathless and laughing to

223

collapse on the bank of spring flowers at the water's edge.

* * *

Hannah murmured, half-waking to a distant memory of the scented golden globe her mother had once shown her how to make from the cowslips that grew in profusion behind their Parkgate cottage. Wasn't there a rhyme? *Tossy-ball, tossy-ball, tell me true . . .*

Before she could complete the simple rhyming couplet of childhood, sleep claimed her once more. So did the dreams. This time they took the form of the jumbled sequences she had known before; a confusion of pictures and snatches of conversation that made little sense and quickly sank to oblivion.

Hannah woke with an aching head to a sultry late-August dawn, midges dancing on the surface of the millpond and an ominous bank of purple storm clouds gathering over the Berwyn hills of Wales.

Swilling her face and hands at the washstand, she reached for her clothes and began to dress, but a sudden wave of dizziness and the need to sit down sent her groping for the edge of the bed. She concentrated on breathing deeply, rubbing her throbbing temple. Thunderstorms always used to induce a sick headache but the problem seemed latterly to have subsided and she had hoped it had become a thing of the past — though recalling the disturbed night, it was hardly surprising that a reaction had set in, she supposed.

The swimming sensation subsided but she sat on a while, pondering on the dream. The woman had looked more at ease with herself than on the last occasion Hannah had seen her.

At Agden churchyard — goodness, it was getting on for three weeks ago now — there had been a severity about her responses to the cleric, a pitiable sense of longing in the later sequence as she had thrown a glance at the book-lined wall of the dim little parlour, as if the weight of duty at having to care for her sister's child had all been too much to bear, when all she had ever asked of life was to be left alone with her books and the learning she found so satisfying.

Hannah had to wonder if her namesake had spent the remainder of her life in a state of disappointment and bitter regret at what fate had flung at her, and yet it had been clear that in her way Hannah Mary had loved the child deeply.

The sound of the millwheel beginning its daily churning brought Hannah back to the present and she frowned, shocked at the power the dreams were having over her. She tried to school her thoughts to practicalities and the day ahead, but her mind strayed relentlessly on.

Cameron, the startling impact of his kiss, its gentleness and the way his beard had warmly brushed her face as his lips had pressed against her brow, the manly smell of horses and honest toil about his person . . . the strength of the arms holding her . . .

She mustn't think of it — must not! The act had been nothing more than an expression of kindness and comfort and even if it had held a deeper meaning, so what? Even to think about it was pointless when neither of them was free.

It struck Hannah with a piercing sorrow that she would never know the meaning of true love; she had forfeited any right to that when she had accepted Edward's offer of marriage.

A distant rumble of thunder brought her abruptly back to reality and she gave herself a mental shake. The family would be assembling for breakfast. They would be wondering where she was. Pushing back her tumbling strands of hair, Hannah pulled herself to her feet and reached for her petticoat.

★   ★   ★

A little later over breakfast, the miller remarked upon her quietness. 'You're looking a bit peaky, too. Blow me, yes. Are you ailing, Hannah?'

'No, no. It's this weather. There's a thunderstorm brewing. They never did agree with me. I get these bad heads when the weather's like this.'

'That sounds like a megrim,' Cameron said, looking up from his heaped plate. 'They're nasty things. Mother used to suffer from them. Feverfew's the stuff to get rid of it. Mother swore by it. She'd steep the leaves in a cup of boiled water and drink it down once it had cooled. Come to think of it I saw a clump in the orchard by the gate. Bear with me a moment, Hannah, and I'll fetch some.'

Before Hannah could protest he had risen from the table and gone, under the astonished gaze of his brothers.

Food for Cameron was regarded with something close to reverence, and his abandoning a meal to go outside and grub about in the grass for a fistful of leaves had them momentarily stunned into silence.

Hannah, putting Cameron's breakfast of fat bacon and fried potatoes on top of the range to keep hot, remembered how Delyth Pennington had provided the same remedy at Croft House. She had been good with herbs, Delyth. She had persuaded her father to let her have a small lobby off the kitchens as a stillroom. How long ago it all seemed now. Hannah almost had to wonder if she really had been wife to an ageing man with five daughters from a previous marriage, four of them wed, the last destined to live at home and be half-sister to any other children that might come along from the new union.

Wife she had been, of course. There was Vinnie, her child, as living proof of it.

Cameron was back shortly with a few delicate fronds of greenery clutched in his fist. He took up the black-iron kettle that hung over the fire and poured water into a cup, dropping in a few sprigs.

'Leave it a minute or two to distil. It

has a bitter taste but 'twill do the trick.'

'Thank you,' Hannah said gratefully, going to the range to retrieve his meal for him.

It was one of many small kindnesses that Cameron had shown her and, breakfast over, with everyone gone about their daily work and thunder muttering in the skies, Hannah was pensive as she gathered up the dirty pots.

At the start of that week Cameron Blake had come to her assistance in a very different way.

The larder shelves had again been running low and at his father's request Cameron had taken her into town to pick up some household items that were too bulky to be transported by hand — a cake of sugar, a keg of malt vinegar, a case of tea and one or two other necessities. She had been about to enter the grocery store on the High Street when a shrill and disturbingly familiar voice had stopped her in her tracks.

'Widow Nightingale's lodger that was? That one's no better than she ought to be! Believe me. I know what I know.'

In the shop, a small group of ladies were gathered together talking. At the head Hannah recognised her old adversary Felicia Black and automatically she darted back into the shadows of the entrance.

'Tell us, do,' one of the women said eagerly.

Three bonneted heads leaned closer and the whispering commenced. Hannah stood, undecided what to do. Evidently this was Miss Black's afternoon off and she had met up with some of her acquaintances while out shopping. The venom in the woman's tone was unmistakable and Hannah, having no doubt that her name was being slated, turned abruptly on her heel and left the premises. Dodging traffic and pedestrians, she retraced her steps across the bustling street and hurried along to the ironmonger's outside which Cameron had found a space to wait with the horse and cart.

'Is there something amiss, Hannah?' he asked in concern, seeing her set face.

'No. I mean . . . well, yes. It is unfortunate, but Miss Black is in the shop with some other ladies. I just didn't think. I am afraid I acted on impulse and came away.'

'Miss Black, you say? Would this be the body that caused you trouble at Lower Dirtwich?'

'Yes, that is correct. I'm sorry, Cameron. You have given up your time to bring me into town. I know you could be better employed — but perhaps if we were to wait a short while, the problem will disperse.'

Cameron gave a disparaging snort and threw the leather reins aside. 'Chances are she'll be in there with her cronies half the morning. Here, give me the grocery list. I'll get the provisions for you.'

'But — '

'No buts. I'll not have you belittled in

front of the whole town,' he raged.

With reluctance Hannah handed over the shopping list. 'Thank you. I shall slip to the butcher's while you are gone. I need to pay the bill.'

*　*　*

There was a queue at the butcher's shop and when Hannah finally emerged, stamping the sawdust off the floor from her boots, she was surprised to find the cart empty of shopping and Cameron evidently still in the grocery store.

She made her way along the street, stopping opposite the shop to see if there was any sign of him.

This was the busiest part of the day and a mother, clutching two large loaves of bread and a shopping basket, and with several children in tow, almost cannoned into her.

'Beg pardon, ma'am,' the mother said, flustered, then had to hastily pass one of the loaves onto Hannah to grab her small boy and prevent him from darting out onto the road under the nose of a passing horse and rider. The gentleman cursed, reining in with a trampling of hooves and a shower of muddy water that liberally splashed the woman from head to foot.

'I am sorry,' said Hannah, passing back the soggy bread that had not escaped a dowsing.

The mother nodded her thanks and hurried her children on, and Hannah, keeping as close to the edge of the road as possible, craned her neck to see what was happening across the way.

Today also happened to be market day and the town was full of herdsmen, tradespeople, merchants and shoppers, all adding to the general clamour and confusion, leaving her struggling to see the shop entrance.

However, there was no mistaking the deep, manly voice raised in argument that boomed through the open doorway of the grocery store, and to Hannah's embarrassment and chagrin she realised that Cameron was most definitely speaking up on her behalf.

'Let me make this clear, Miss Black. Mistress Morgan happens to be in our employment at Overton Mill. She has been for some time now and her continued wellbeing and peace of mind rests with us. I don't mind admitting that her presence at the millhouse is the best thing that's happened to our family in many a while.'

'Is that so?' the woman sneered. 'What an effect a pretty face can have!'

'Madam, my father is a man of shrewd business sense and a ripe judge of character to boot,' Cameron continued levelly. 'In other words, he knows a trustworthy face when he sees one. If he had had the slightest question of doubt as to the lady's character he would not have taken her on at the mill. And let that be an end to it.'

Felicia Black, however, was not to be silenced.

'She had a trusted position in the office at my place of work, I tell you.

She abused it,' she said tightly.

'Stuff and nonsense! If you're trying to make an untrue accusation, I should think again. Slanderous comments can be construed as libel in a court of law, remember.'

'Are you suggesting I am telling an untruth, sir?' she raged.

There was indignation in the voice but also a note of qualm, and Cameron was quick to spot it. 'If there was an error in the books,' he said, deadly quiet, 'then the finger has to be pointed elsewhere. I wonder where, mistress?'

Silence. The listening women shuffled their feet uneasily, their cheeks coloured.

Into the stillness came a discreet cough from the shopkeeper. 'Cameron, your order is put together and waiting. Will I help you load up the cart?'

'My thanks, Wilbur. I'd appreciate it.' Cameron turned abruptly to face the now still group. 'Well then, ladies, I'll bid you all good morning.'

He hoisted the large keg of malt vinegar onto his shoulder as if it were no heavier than a sack of feathers and left the shop. He crossed the road to where Hannah stood, her cheeks burning, and giving her a wink of encouragement, suggested they went to see if the horse was still where he had left it.

Struggling to regain her composure, her head reeling, she followed him along the street to where the animal was making full use of the rest and had fallen into a doze, head down and ears slack.

'You stay here while we see to the loading up,' he said to Hannah, dumping the keg down on the bed of the cart. 'We'll not be long. Then we can go.'

Hannah put out a restraining hand. 'Cameron, I heard what was said. I should thank you. I am only sorry you had to get involved in this unseemly business.'

'There's nothing to be sorry about. It's all a gossip like that one deserves — a dose of her own medicine. I doubt if Miss Black will be spreading any more of her poison. Not in this particular case, anyhow.' Taking her hand, he guided her over to the side of the cart. 'Here, let me help you aboard. There we are. All right?'

As the men were loading up the cart, Hannah spotted the women leaving the shop, scuttling away in different directions with their heads bowed.

As they set off, she could not suppress a gurgle of unexpected laughter when Cameron doffed his cap jovialiy to one of them as they passed by.

★　★　★

The interlude played on her mind later and, appreciative though she was of Cameron Blake's solicitude, Hannah was bothered by it.

The fact remained that he was promised to Lizzie Marsh, and the young woman might be justified at taking umbrage at matters that could come between them. Hannah was already less than popular with Lizzie. Too much attention on her betrothed's part, no matter how innocent, could only provoke additional cause for complaint — and that was the last thing Hannah wanted.

Thunder rumbled again as the storm crept closer and there was a sudden flash and crackle of lightning. The cat shot in through the open door and leaped for the dark safety of the curtained recess by the fireplace to hide until the worst of the weather had passed.

Hannah pressed her fingers to her forehead. The feverfew was doing its work; the pain was receding and she was thankful, but she wished the storm would finally break. She never had liked them.

As she washed the greasy pots, she came to the conclusion that the only answer to the situation with Cameron was to play down any future attention — truly play it down, and not allow the nudging spark she felt between them any fuel for flame. It was not going to be easy.

Mid-morning arrived and the storm had still not broken. Assembling the customary repast of strong ale for dust-parched throats on a battered tin tray, Hannah saw that Cameron was at work on the forecourt and seized the opportunity to put her scheme to the test. She was crossing the cobblestones with the ale when Cameron paused from his labours to enquire after her headache, as she had known he would.

Hannah was deliberately abrupt. 'Thank you, the condition has passed.'

'Did the remedy help, then?' Cameron enquired, relieving her of one of the frothing tankards of ale whilst looking at her questioningly.

'Yes, I think so.'

'That's good to hear. Wonderful stuff, fever few. Mother swore by it.'

'Yes, you said.'

'If there was anything she made sure and grew in the garden it was that.

Amazing, how these things work.'

'It is indeed.' She broke off. 'Cameron, you must excuse me. I really cannot stand around talking. The master and your brothers will want their drinks and I must attend to the weekly accounts while I have an hour to spare.'

Cameron, however, was not to be put off. He took a long swig of ale before adding, 'You'll strain your eyes poring over those ledgers. It's the last thing you need after a megrim. I seem to recall Mother going to lie down and rest. Here, give me those drinks. I'll take them across and you go in and sit down for a little while.'

'Please don't fuss, Cameron. I told you. I am feeling perfectly well now.'

Hating the hurt look on the bearded face that turned swiftly to bafflement, she continued on her way. The puzzled gaze was still on her as she reached the mill and it was with relief that she stepped inside and closed the door.

* * *

Books finally attended to — it took longer than usual since, contrary to her words, the indisposition had left her feeling fuddled and wrung out — she had to steel herself to keep up the pretence when she took the ledger for Cameron to check.

She need not have worried, since he had obviously taken the hint. Passing his eye over the neat columns of figures, he handed the book back with nothing more than a brief smile to indicate that he had no quibbles with the work.

'Thank you,' Hannah said quietly.

She despised herself for treating him this way but what else could she do under the circumstances? Lizzie would have no complaints, she thought with a wry little twist of her lips. She rather suspected that Lizzie Marsh would have been secretly delighted to have witnessed the Malpas scene that had caused Hannah such distress.

Soon afterwards the storm broke and the day ended in downpour. Beyond the door the rain fell in soaking capfuls and Hannah, for want of something to stop her brooding, surveyed the millhouse floor. The constant traffic of booted feet had transported the usual slurry of grain bits and dust to the flagstones, and the addition of globs of mud from Will's recent visit had made matters a good deal worse. Lips tightening, Hannah mustered up some final shreds of energy and went to the copper to fill a pail with hot water to deal with the mess.

By evening the rain had stopped. Resisting the urge to sit by the kitchen fire with her feet up after what had been a trying day, Hannah slipped over to Cuddington. She wished to question Madge about the journal. Aware of the need to be circumspect, she composed what she was going to say as she plodded through the puddles to Brook Cottage.

She found Madge in the yard, showing Vinnie a butterfly.

'Come on in,' she said, leading the way. 'You're looking peaky, daughter.

I'm not surprised after the storm we've had. We were getting in the potatoes when it started, weren't we, Vinnie? We had to leave off and shelter. What a din! And the lightning! I feared we'd get struck.'

'Was Vinnie frightened?'

'Not her! 'Twould take more than that to scare our Vinnie, wouldn't it, my lambkin?'

The child laughed and pointed to the cat on the hearth. The little tabby had produced a litter of kittens in the loft above the stable. She had recently brought them out and they now tumbled about her on the hearth, pouncing and playing.

'Cat!' Vinnie said gleefully. 'Kitty-cat!'

'Clever girl,' Hannah said proudly. She looked at Madge. 'She'll be fluent by the year end at this rate.'

'It's true. Bright as a button, she is. But then you only have to know her mam to see where she gets her brains from — and her looks, come to that.

She'll break a few hearts when she's older, that one.'

Hannah subsided onto a stool, glad to take the weight off her feet, while Madge busied herself with kettle and pots.

'Madge,' Hannah began, once both woman were sitting with the tea-things displayed around them. 'I wonder if you could tell me something.'

'I'll do my best.' Madge poured milk for Vinnie, handing it to the child with a warning not to spill it. 'What was it you wanted to know?'

'I've come across an old journal. It was written by Miller Blake's mother.'

Madge nodded. 'That would be Sarah Jane. She didn't make old bones.'

'So I believe. Madge, she writes about a friend who visited. I have an idea it was the person that used to come here with a small child. I think I mentioned it before when I spoke about those dreams I kept having.'

A guarded look came over Madge's face. 'You know I don't hold with all that jiggery-pokery. There's no such thing as dreaming into the past.'

'Very well. Let us stick to the facts. Do you know who they might have been?'

'Daughter, there's been endless comings and goings at Brook Cottage over the years. My man was at everyone's beck and call; never could see an end to his working day at times. Many's the night I've kept the supper hot while he mended a boot with the owner stood peg-legged on the yard with one foot clad only in a sock!'

'I thought the woman's name was Annie but I was mistaken. It was the same as mine,' Hannah said with caution.

'Hannah, you mean?' Madge frowned, thoughts chasing across her nut-brown eyes. 'Just a minute. It's coming back to me. There was a Hannah that used to call, 'tis many years ago now. Lots of water gone under the bridge since then and my memory isn't as sharp as it used to be.

Hannah . . . Jane, was it? No, that was Hannah Rawlings that was. Hannah Mary, that's it! Fancy me forgetting that, and her a Carraway too!'

Hannah's heart crashed about within the tight lacing of her stays. She took a sip of tea to try and steady her nerves. 'Do you remember if she lived at Agden?'

'Why, yes, she did, come to think of it. She rented a little house off the green. I seem to recall a branch of the Carraways had lived there at one time. There'd been some sort of tragedy if I remember rightly. The sister had died and Hannah Mary took on the young child as her ward. I don't know anything about the father, though.'

'According to the journal he had left the wife before the child was born.'

'That figures. Happen that was what drew Hannah Mary to Agden after what happened to the sister. Clean sweep, so to speak. There was a big age gap between the two of them. 'Twould have been hard for a spinster, I'm

247

thinking. She came across as being a bookish lady, not the sort to relish having a child at her skirts. But all credit to the woman, she made a good fist of bringing the little girl up.'

Hannah was confused. What did Madge mean by her words? Where had Hannah Mary come from originally if it was not Agden? Madge was looking at her as if she suspected a reason behind all this that was beyond mere curiosity, and Hannah had to draw back a little. 'I wonder why she visited Brook Cottage,' she said, keeping her tone light though her mind teemed with unanswered questions.

'Didn't I say? There was a blood tie, way, way back.'

'A . . . a blood tie?' Hannah was finding it hard to breathe. 'Madge, are you sure?'

'Sure as can be. 'Twas very distant, you understand. Hannah Mary knew of it, though. Not one for calling on all and sundry, was Hannah Mary, and I wouldn't say the visits here were frequent. Edge, my name was before I married. The Carraway link came through my grandmother.'

'So you're an Agden girl.'

'Bless you, Hannah, no. We Edges are Wrenbury folk, same as the Carraways.'

'Wrenbury?' Hannah frowned. 'I don't know of it.'

'It's a tidy village on the road to Nantwich. Hannah Mary never spoke of it. Close, she was. What you'd call a private person. Some things you'd never ask.'

'Did she live out her days at Agden, do you know?'

'Now that I can answer. When the girl grew up and married, Hannah Mary gave up the Agden house and went back to where she'd come from. That was the last I heard of her. She'll be long gone now, of course.'

By this time Hannah's heart was pounding so loudly she felt her friend must surely hear. 'Is it far to Wrenbury?' she asked.

'Not really. Maybe an hour in the

trap . . . Daughter, you're never thinking of going there?'

'I . . . I don't know. Probably not.'

Hannah swallowed hard. It was almost too much to take in. Her hands were shaking and the teacup in the saucer rattled and she put it down. Madge took a bite of fruit cake, chewing on it thoughtfully.

'Funny you should come across Sarah Jane's book. Does it say much about the life she led at the millhouse?'

'A little. She mentions the job she had in keeping down the flour-dust. I know how she felt!'

'I'm sure. Did I ever say how the Blakes were connected with the Nightingales?'

'No!' Hannah'stared at Madge. The situation was becoming more bizarre by the minute! 'Connected in what way?'

'Oh, as I understand it 'twas through one of the Beeston cousins. Again it's a very distant link. That would be on my late husband's side, of course. Small world, isn't it?'

'Very,' Hannah answered expressively.

Her mind struggled to take in all she had learned. Here she had been these lonely months, thinking she had no one to call her own when all the while there was a relative right here before her; her dear friend Madge Nightingale. Hannah could hardly credit it. All right, so the link was tenuous. Yet it was there, and it made a difference to how she felt.

Madge collected up the tea-things and took them through to the scullery and with Vinnie occupied with the kittens at her feet, Hannah gave herself up to thought. It almost beggared belief that her great-aunt Hannah Mary had come to this very house and brought her mother here as a child, and even more amazing was the fact that they had visited the mill as well. That she should find herself beset by dreams of the past now gave the matter credence. Coming here must have acted as the trigger purported by the wise-woman during a casual meeting many years ago on the Parkgate estuary. It had also become clear why no trace of Hannah's forebears existed hereabouts. With the family based elsewhere, the mystery was solved.

'Kitty-cat!' Vinnie lisped, reaching out to stroke a black and white ball of fluff.

Madge, returning to the houseplace, was ever watchful of the child. 'Gently, now. Kittens have sharp claws. Mind he doesn't scratch you.' She broke off, straightening, and fixed Hannah with a disturbingly piercing look. 'The child you spoke of. I've just remembered. Her name was Alice. She'd play with the kittens just as our Vinnie is doing. What an extraordinary tool the memory is.'

'Yes,' Hannah murmured. 'It is.'

Her heart sang as she headed back along the lane in the gathering dusk. To have found out what she had wanted to know was satisfying enough, but the added knowledge that she was no longer alone in the world was unbelievable!

It bothered her that she could not share the discovery with her friend Madge, though nothing could cloud the pleasure of this special moment and she hugged it to her joyfully, her delight lending her wings.

At the mill, Will was in the field schooling a wayward horse. Hannah sent him a wave and made to carry on to the house, but the boy gave a shout.

'Hannah, wait!' He came cantering up the fence and reined in, the horse prancing and sidling and snorting fearsomely. Soothing it with a murmur, he went on, 'Hannah, you've a caller. I would have come to fetch you but you can see what a handful this fellow is. He needs teaching some manners before I'd trust him out on the roads.'

'A caller? For me?' Hannah was conscious of all her newfound joy draining from her. Was this it, the moment she had always dreaded? She swallowed hard, hanging on to the hope that there was some terrible mistake. 'Are you sure, Will?'

'Yes, absolutely. The person turned up just after you'd gone to Brook Cottage. I think — '

Hannah heard no more. She was already speeding towards the house, her stomach churning.

Someone had shown the visitor into the front parlour. She stood up as Hannah entered the room.

'Hannah,' she said softly. 'Thank goodness I've found you.'

It was her step-daughter, Delyth Pennington.

13

'Delyth!' Hannah's hands went to her face in shock. 'But . . . what are you doing here? Edward — Does he know — '

'Papa is ailing,' Delyth cut in. 'Hannah, please, you have to come home.'

Hannah's legs went weak. She managed to traverse the faded Turkey carpet and flopped down on to the sofa, oblivious for once to the scratchiness of the horsehair covering.

Taking her lead, Delyth Pennington moved to sit opposite. She was a slight young woman, plain of face apart from a pair of truly beautiful grey eyes that were currently shadowed with worry and concern.

'Hannah, please. You must listen to me. Papa is very ill. The doctor fears for his life.'

Hannah stared, unable to take the words in. All she could think of was that here was an end to all her hopes and struggles. Those demoralising hours at the salt mine, toiling and slaving in appalling conditions until she had wanted to lie down in a ditch and die, all to no avail. The worry over her child, the constant dread of the knock on the door that would portend discovery, the sly looks and taunts she had endured, the sheer effort involved in carrying on, day after day . . .

'How did you find me?' she asked in a voice that was devoid of expression.

'It was quite by chance,' Delyth Pennington replied. 'I was shopping in the market place. The gypsies were there. You know how they turn up from time to time? One of them approached me and I bought a sprig of lucky heather from her — well, 'tis said to be bad luck to turn a gypsy away. She wanted to tell my fortune like they do. I dislike the way they press you, it's so humiliating, and this time I resisted but she caught my arm and said she knew something that would benefit me greatly and others too. A look in her eye made me hesitate.'

Delyth moistened her lips and Hannah waited, her face bleached of colour.

'It turned out that the previous autumn she and her man had come across a young woman and baby on the road. The woman was exhausted and footsore and the child was crying pitifully. They took them into their wagon and cared for them. It seemed more than just coincidence and I questioned her further.' Delyth Pennington made a little face. 'It took all the contents of my purse to wheedle the truth out of her!'

So it was the Romany wife who had given her away! As Hannah listened, she became vaguely conscious of a change in the speaker. Delyth Pennington had been a mouse of a girl but now it seemed that enforced circumstances had brought out a hidden strength, and a grudging admiration for her fought with panic at the plight Delyth's coming had put her in.

Dejected and frowning, Hannah struggled to take in the information that had led to her discovery.

'The Romany folk are a strange people, are they not?' Delyth went on. 'I cannot begin to guess how this one singled me out. Maybe it was something about my speech that caused her to make the connection, a similarity perhaps. After all, you and I shared the same governess. It was Violet Sharp that Papa called upon to instruct you in the art of conversation, was it not?'

Hannah nodded, shrugging, stunned into silence at the workings of the hand of fate.

'Then again, 'tis said that the travelling folk are blessed with a second sight. Perhaps it was that.'

'Does anyone else know you are here?' Hannah croaked, finding her voice at last.

'No. It was a long shot and I did not

wish to raise false hopes. After you left, we searched everywhere. Papa was demented. I think he blamed himself for having driven you away, though he never actually said as much.'

'No, well, your father is a proud man.'

'There is that, though his concern was genuine. Hannah, if Papa's actions were anything to go by he thought a great deal of you and still does. He had a fleet of men ride out to search for you and the babe. He even had them drag the lake in case the two of you had met your end there. He wouldn't let the matter rest. But every turn he made, there was nothing. You had both vanished as surely as if you had never existed. In the end it was generally assumed that you had taken Vinnie for an airing on the marshes and perished. It was common knowledge how you loved to walk there with the babe, and the autumn tides can be treacherous.'

'I knew the tides well enough,' Hannah countered. 'I learned them at my father's knee. He was a fisherman. Right from the start he instilled within me how crucial it was to know the movements of the sea and to respect its moods.'

'He sounded a wise man. Hannah, I did not go along with what they said for one moment. You were always too mindful of Vinnie's safety, for one thing.'

She paused. Hannah's gaze fell on the tea tray at the girl's elbow. Someone had thought to provide refreshments — Cameron, probably. He had used the everyday blue and white crockery and found the plum cake she had made only yesterday, slicing it into slabs more suited to tea-time at the mill than serving to a member of the Parkgate gentry. She noticed with a pang that he must have gone upstairs to raid the oaken coffer on the landing for one of the embroidered linen table napkins that his mother had worked for best.

'Papa was beside himself. It must have brought home to him how unbearable he had made life for you, and that what happened was his fault.'

'It was not only that. There was another . . . complication.' Hannah drew a breath, straightening her shoulders. 'Edward is ill, you say? He was always such a robust man.'

'It happened suddenly. He was at the boatyard going over the plans for a new vessel with a customer and he had a seizure. Doctor Gilchrist says it is his heart. Poor Papa. I know how difficult he can be but he is not a bad man, not really. He does not deserve any of this.'

A tear spilled over, running down Delyth's pale cheek. She reached into her reticule for a handkerchief.

'It is bad, then,' Hannah said flatly.

'Very. He is not expected to last the year out. Hannah, he's asking for you. At first he was rambling and I did not take what he said seriously, but now his mind is clearer and still he asks. I do not think he ever believed you were dead, any more than I did. He is talking of renewing the search.'

261

'Oh?' Alarm frisked through Hannah. Having her escorted back to Croft House in disgrace like a runaway child was typical of Edward's modus operandi.

'It is all right,' the girl said hastily, clearly interpreting the matter. 'With Papa indisposed, the running of the household and other matters have fallen to me. I was able to hold things back until I could make investigations of my own.'

'I always thought that the running of the household was Mrs Bell's prerogative,' remarked Hannah, momentarily distracted.

'Oh, fie to Mrs Bell! She can be something of a harridan, can she not? She did not give you an easy time, I fear.'

'Put it this way. She will not take kindly to seeing me again, that is certain.'

'But you will come? If I promise to speak with Mrs Bell, with all the servants; tell them I want every respect, and that not a single word relating to what has happened is to be uttered outside the house, will you come back with me?'

Hannah raised her hands in mute protest and let them drop again to her lap. 'I do not actually have the choice, do I?' she replied in a low voice. 'Edward is my wedded husband. It was remiss of me to do what I did.'

'Hannah, perhaps you were not in your right mind. It is said that when a woman has newly had a child — '

'I knew what I was doing well enough. I was worried for Vinnie, 'tis true. Your father was so hostile towards her. She would have had a miserable existence under his roof — or so it seemed; having to be kept out of sight all the while, the subject of dislike and ridicule just because she was not born a boy. It was more than I could bear. I had to get away. I had to give my child a chance of the happiness she deserved. As to myself . . . I needed peace of mind.'

'And did you find it?'

Hannah shook her head. 'No, not if I'm truthful. What I did has haunted me. Not a day has passed but I have been reminded of it in some form.' She drew another breath. 'How have you come? Did you travel by steam train?'

'Only as far as Chester. The line ends there. I had to take the Stage to Malpas. I have an overnight bag with me, though I have not been able to find a room anywhere. None of the inns in the town would entertain taking a woman traveller.'

'I know,' Hannah said ruefully. 'You are likely to have stood a better chance at Chester. There are some boarding houses there for gentlewomen.'

'I never thought. I did not really want to waste time looking for accommodation. I made enquiries as to where you were — discreetly, I might add — and here I am.'

In the silence that followed, Hannah reflected on how the girl had once befriended her. Delyth had been the only one in that vast, inhospitable house to do so and Hannah now felt she owed her something in return.

'You must stay here tonight,' she said. 'I keep a bed made up in the guest room. It won't be what you are accustomed to and the millwheel can be noisy in the early morning, but you will find it comfortable enough.'

'Are you sure it won't be an imposition, Hannah? Surely there must be somewhere in the town that will take a lone traveller like myself,' Delyth protested.

'It is not likely, or so I discovered to my cost when I first arrived here — though I allow my situation was not the same.'

'Nevertheless, in this day and age one would expect to be able to find a room for the night. Being refused simply because of one's gender is absurd, and not everyone travels under the patronage of a chaperone,' the girl answered spiritedly. 'But there. Malpas is an attractive town, is it not? It has a quaintness all its own. I confess I had never heard of it before now. You would not imagine what a task I had to find its whereabouts. What inspired you to come here, of all places?'

'It was my mother's girlhood home. Or so I believed. I have since discovered that she actually resided at another place not far from here.'

'So your mama was a country woman. I never knew much about your background.'

'No. I was discouraged from speaking of it. Yet there was nothing about my upbringing to be ashamed of. My father was an honest man and Mother was intelligent and hard-working. It wasn't her fault that we fell upon hard times.'

'I'm sure it was not.' The visitor threw a glance around the room at the gleaming rustic furniture and the small attempts at gentility that were a throwback to the late mistress of the house. The buttoned sofa, the fragile china that took an age to dust, the carpet that had probably come to them second-hand at a sale but was quality nonetheless. 'You've evidently landed on your feet here. The miller and his sons seem good folk.'

'Yes, they are. I was fortunate to get a position with them. It was not always the case. Vinnie is being fostered by a widow woman at a village called Cuddington, a little way on from here. Madge Nightingale has been a godsend.' The headache was back with a vengeance and Hannah pressed the back of her hand to her forehead. 'But you must be exhausted. Will I show you to your room? You will want to refresh yourself.'

'Thank you.' Delyth rose to her feet.

Hannah too stood up. 'I must warn you that we live simply here. The boys — that is, Miller Blake's sons — do not exactly stand on ceremony.'

'It is of no import,' Delyth said. 'Hannah, I take it the Blakes know nothing of this? What will you tell them?'

'I don't know. The truth; it will have

to be. I shall have to ponder on what to say.' Hannah paused. What would they think of her? What would Cameron's reaction be? All this, on top of how she had treated him! Dear Lord, he would probably never want to set eyes on her again and she could not blame him. Her heart constricting painfully, for she could not bear the idea of being the object of his scorn, she went on, 'It might be best to approach Miller Blake. I shall wait until after supper, when there is a better chance of catching him alone.'

'As you think best. Hannah, have you thought how you will introduce me? A friend from the past, perhaps?'

'Yes. Yes. Well then, shall we go? I am sorry you were kept waiting. I went to see Vinnie.'

'Yes, the young man who brought the tea said as much. What a very big man he is.'

'That would be Cameron. He has a fine singing voice,' Hannah said.

How strange that she should think of

that. It struck her that she would never hear it again, ringing out as Cameron went about his daily work.

Indicating for Delyth to follow, Hannah crossed the room, picked up the valise that stood by the wall and, opening the door, stood back for her guest to pass through.

★   ★   ★

'So that is all,' Hannah said some time later. She met the miller's bewildered face levelly. 'I am no widow. I am a married woman and I am sorry I let you think otherwise — truly sorry.'

There was a long silence while the information she had revealed was digested.

Cameron, standing with his back to the fire, looked withdrawn. Hannah had not been able to catch the miller alone and she tried not to let her gaze dwell on the still frame and shadowed face.

'It was not my intention to deliberately mislead,' she said when the silence became unendurable. 'I had no definite plan when I came to the town. I simply wanted to be where my mother had known happiness and thought I may find it too. There was my daughter to consider. The story that I was a widow . . . it — '

'Came about by assumption,' Cameron said, coming to her rescue. 'Well, that's to be expected.'

'So what happens now? Will you go back?' the miller asked somewhat bluntly.

'What choice have I?' Hannah heard the tremor in her voice and struggled to control it. 'Edward is my husband. I should have been there when he took ill. It was weakness that made me run off like that.'

'Nay, nay,' the miller said. 'You were nobbut a girl with a young babe to protect. You felt stifled and unwanted. 'Twas a brave thing you did.' He rubbed his face with his fist, coughing a little, clearly flummoxed by the situation. ''Tis a pretty pickle and no mistake. Do we tell the boys? Or would you prefer to keep it from them?'

'They'll not tattle,' Cameron assured. 'There'll be nothing said outside these four walls.'

'You are most kind. It is more than I deserve. Perhaps it is only fair that Thomas and Will should be told the full story. Madge Nightingale, too. I shall attend to that myself. Thank you, both of you, for being so understanding.'

Miller Blake brushed her words aside. 'We shall miss you, lass. Blow me, yes.'

'Aye, we shall,' Cameron said heavily. He met her gaze and Hannah saw such unhappiness there that she wanted to offer words of comfort. Only there was no comfort. Not for Cameron, not for the rest of the family and certainly not for herself.

'Tis a lonely road you travel, rawnie.

The Romany wife's words came back to her almost as if they had been spoken aloud and she gave her head a little shake as if to clear it. Some inner

271

sense told her that she was far from reaching the end of that road as yet, though nothing would have convinced her that the route would lead back to the place she had found so abhorrent. Her one consolation was the fact that in her heart, she knew she was doing the right thing.

Confession over, she excused herself to go and attend to their guest.

★　★　★

Twenty-four hours later, she was gone.

'The place isn't the same without her,' Thomas said, as they gathered around the table at supper time. Cutting himself a piece of cheese and a hunk of bread, he added an onion from the platter and bit into it with a crunch that made the eyes water.

Already the kitchen wore a neglected air. The floor, ever Hannah's bane, bore the marks of flour-trodden boots and mud. The supper table was carelessly set and the black-iron stove, always gleaming, had not received its morning black-leading. The cat sat yowling forlornly before it, since no one had thought to feed her. The sound epitomised the feelings of all those around the table.

'I've told Sally she's gone,' Thomas continued.

His father looked up sharply. 'You didn't give away any details, did you?'

'Of course not. Though I'd trust Sally with my life. I said Hannah had been unexpectedly called to the place she had come from and left it at that, the way we agreed.'

The miller nodded his approval, chomping on a crust of bread. It crossed his mind to wonder when again they would know the benefit of decent meals.

'I've been thinking, boys.' He threw the gloomy faces around the table a quick glance. 'What happened to Hannah has altered my perspective on certain issues. Aye, she struck me as being a staunch young woman. Not one to give up easily. She must have been sorely tried to forsake her marriage and leave what must have been a comfortable existence for the insecurities of having to fend for herself. Oh, I know what she said. She found life under her husband's roof intolerable. But she was safe and well provided for. There'll be many a woman would have settled for that.'

Faces were mystified, his sons wondering what might be coming next.

'Thomas, do you still have this yen to be a seafarer?'

'Aye, I do, Father. And what's more, my Sally's reconciled to the idea.'

'Oh, it's 'my Sally' now, is it?' A glimmer of humour appeared in his father's gaze. 'That's a turn-up for the books, that is.'

'We want to be betrothed. It was something Hannah said that changed Sally's mind. Seems they'd had a heart-to-heart.'

'Hannah gave me one of those an' all,' Will mumbled, two spots of colour heightening his cheekbones. 'It went something along the lines of not wasting talents and putting energies into what a fellow's good at.'

'Like breaking horses before they break you?' the miller said. 'You can't deny it. D'you think I've not noticed the miscellany of nags that've been eating their heads off in my stable? The oat bin's never needed so much filling up!'

'I'll pay, Father. You can dock it from my wage.'

'Nay, lad. I was but jesting. Make use of the fodder and welcome. Just have a care for yourself, that's all I ask.'

By this time the three brothers were sitting back in their chairs, alert for the next revelation. They did not have to wait long for it.

'Thomas,' the miller said, his face working with effort. 'I've given what I'm about to say a great deal of thought and I've come to a decision. Well, I kept thinking of that poor wretch back at Parkgate, wondering what had happened to his wife and child when they'd gone seemingly without trace. If I have to have sleepless nights I'd prefer it not to be for the same reason. Go ahead and pursue your dream, lad. Go with my blessing.'

Confusion, bewilderment and then sheer joy crossed Thomas's face in swift succession. He stood up, chair scraping on the stone flags of the floor, and reached for his jerkin.

'Where are you off to?' the miller growled.

'To tell Sally. Father, I can never thank you enough.'

He went, leaving his half-eaten meal and gently steaming mug of tea. Will, shrugging, resumed his supper.

No one had noticed that during the whole of the discourse Cameron had not uttered a single word. He pushed aside his uneaten meal and followed his brother out, slamming the door behind him. Soon afterwards the millwheel could be heard, grinding the first of the new-season corn. No singing. Whatever his problem, he was taking solace in work, a move that the miller knew only too well.

14

Croft House stood on a high rise of land overlooking the Dee Estuary. Not especially large as houses go, it was nevertheless an imposing structure, porticoed and deep-windowed, built on the classical lines of several decades before. Protected from the prevailing winds by a stand of pines, it had a rose garden and a small lake and was considered one of the better houses of the district.

Hannah's heart quailed as the carriage travelled up the drive between flanks of tall elms whose tired foliage told of the cessation of summer.

Time had been of the essence, but she was glad she had snatched some moments to sponge and press her kerseymere and dress her hair in a more elaborate style than the one adopted as housekeeper to a miller.

Vinnie was wearing her best frock of cheap cotton, much be-frilled and tucked, that had looked so becoming in the cottage kitchen but now felt not quite the thing for the daughter of Edward Pennington.

Delyth had sent a wire to inform the house of their coming and the servants were lined up in the hallway to welcome their mistress back into the fold. At their head, important in rustling black, house-keys jangling on a chain at her waist, was housekeeper Mrs Bell.

'Take heart,' Delyth whispered, pressing Hannah's arm.

Inwardly doubting that her presence here would ever be accepted, Hannah held her head high and met the housekeeper's boot-button gaze with a steely challenge, before sweeping on and mounting the wide staircase. Vinnie, clasped in her arms, was awed for once into silence.

When they reached the first floor landing the two young women parted company.

'Your rooms are prepared, madam,' the housekeeper said, having followed behind.

'Thank you, Mrs Bell. Please have some hot water sent up. After I have refreshed myself I shall go and see the master.'

'Very well, madam. Shall you require the maid?'

'Thank you, no. I shall ring when I am ready.'

In her bedchamber someone had lit a fire, for the day was cool. Despite the housekeeper's assurances, the room felt unused and neglected. Swiftly Hannah attended to her own and her child's ablutions, after which she summoned the maid to be escorted to her husband.

'Will I take the infant from you, ma'am?' the girl offered. She was new to Hannah; a fresh-faced girl with dimples and a roguish twinkle. Hannah was pleased to see that she had none of the sourness of her predecessor.

'Not just yet. I shall take Vinnie with me. Perhaps later on she can go to the nursery. I don't know you, do I? What is your name?' she asked.

'Hopley, ma'am. Susan Hopley. I'm from Neston. My da's a miner there.' The girl dipped a curtsey.

'Oh, I see. And am I right in assuming that you are my personal maid?'

'I don't know, ma'am. I do anything that's asked. Mrs Bell sent me up when you rang.'

'Then I shall speak to her later. I shall need someone to attend me. I think you and I will get on.'

'Yes'm. Thank you, ma'am.' She curtseyed again, cap-frills bobbing furiously. 'The master is along this way . . . but you'll know that already.'

Hannah was directed along the thickly-carpeted corridor to her husband's suite of rooms on the north side of the house. Tapping lightly, the maidservant entered the room and announced the visitor.

'That will be all, Susan. You may now go.'

'Yes'm.'

Hannah, astonished at how readily the orders had tripped off her tongue, waited until the door had closed before approaching the high, curtained bed.

It was a gloomy chamber panelled in dark wood and furnished along sternly masculine lines in heavily carved mahogany. The hangings of plum-coloured velour were half drawn across the windows and at first the figure in the bed was not easy to make out. Once her eyes adjusted to the dimness, however, Hannah could not contain her shock at the difference in the man she had called husband.

Gone was the jowly, ruddy appearance. In its place was a pale shadow of Edward's former self and her stomach constricted in pity. His eyes were closed, his breathing shallow. He was supported by many bolsters and his eyes were closed. She wondered if he was sleeping.

'Edward?' she said softly, sitting down in the chair beside the bed and arranging Vinnie on her lap.

The eyes blinked open; a scowl appeared. 'Well, my wife? So you've taken it upon yourself to come back!' The attempt at a rebuke failed utterly and in the next instant Edward Pennington's face crumpled. 'Hannah. My dearest love, how I've wanted you here.'

Vinnie, in Hannah's arms, chose that moment to reach out to a decoration of embroidered flowers on the bedcover and Edward noticed her as if for the first time. 'The child. How she has grown. Is she forward for her age?'

'Very much so. She was walking before her first year was out and she is already forming words.' Hannah broke off. 'Edward, I am sorry.'

'No, no, it is I who should be delivering the apology. I was boorish and unkind and that was very wrong. Can you ever forgive me?'

'You are ailing. Perhaps you were not yourself at the time.'

'I had this pain on and off, it is true.

Indigestion, I thought. It can make a man ill-tempered. The doctor tells me it is my heart playing up.'

'Oh, Edward, you should have said. How are you now?'

He smiled grimly and said in his strange new breathless voice, 'As you see, I am not a well man. Though I am all the better for seeing my wife and small daughter. What a pretty creature she is, so like her mama. Hannah, you are staying?' he added anxiously.

'I . . . yes.'

'I am so very, very glad . . . '

His eyelids drooped. He gave a little sigh and lapsed into sleep. Hannah waited, and when he showed no sign of waking she took a firm hold of the child and arose and quietly left.

* * *

Settling in again at Croft House was far from easy. Hannah was constantly aware of the averted eyes of the staff and could only guess at the tattle that went on below stairs. Added to which, although her stepdaughter's 'talking to' had gone part way to making Mrs Bell less corrosive, the housekeeper was hardly her most gracious.

'Mock turtle, Madam?' Mrs Bell frowned over the week's menu that she had been presented with. 'I had thought Scotch broth for Monday.'

'The master is partial to mock turtle, Mrs Bell. Doctor Gilchrist has insisted that he is to be fed his favourite dishes, providing they are not too heavy — which I am sure they would not be,' Hannah added, thinking to soften the housekeeper.

Mrs Bell's face remained impassive. 'I shall speak with Cook, madam.'

'Please do not trouble yourself. I shall do it myself. In fact, in future it might be best if I am the one to consult with Cook over the weekly menus. I am sure you have more than enough to occupy your time as it is. This will be one thing less for you to see to.'

'Very well, madam.' The woman's

tone was cutting.

'And while I think on, I wish to have Susan Hopley for my maid. She is new here, I believe.'

'Yes, madam. Decks left to get wed. Hopley is her replacement. She came on the best authority from the vicarage at Neston. She's willing enough, but madam, I should point out that she has no training as a lady's maid.'

'No matter. I like the girl and that is the main thing. Another thing. When you are interviewing for a nanny for my daughter, be sure and let me know. I wish to be present myself. Do I make that clear?'

'Yes, madam.'

The housekeeper curtseyed and left the room, disapproval in every line of her body.

Once the door had closed on her Hannah breathed out a sigh and Delyth, seated in the window embrasure ostensibly concentrating on her embroidery, gave a chuckle.

'That was telling her! What a great

deal you have learned during your absence, Hannah.'

'Maybe I have merely grown up. A stint at a salt mine is enough to knock the corners off anyone!'

'Did you really labour alongside the mine-women? I cannot imagine how it must have been. Winter, too. Were you not cold?' Delyth questioned.

'All the while, tired and aching too. It was far worse than gutting fish on the quayside and I thought that abhorrent at the time. Still, one survives. I did not have the sort of upbringing that you and your sisters enjoyed, remember.'

'You were not roughly reared, Hannah. You have a genteel manner about you.'

'Mother made sure of that. As to the rest, your father went to great pains to see that I was adequately instructed to take my place in society.'

'Yes, I remember. Hannah, how do you find Papa?'

'Oh, weak and ailing. He is going to

require a great deal of nursing. We can probably manage for now but I think we may need professional help as time goes on. It might be best to ask the doctor if he can recommend someone.'

'That is a good idea. You must make sure and spend time with little Vinnie. What a darling she is. Is she happy in the nursery with Susan?'

'Perfectly. She is not a difficult child to please and Susan tells me she has younger brothers and sisters, so she is used to little ones.'

A tap on the door announced the return of Mrs Bell with the news that the dressmaker had arrived to measure madam for new winter gowns.

'Tell her I shall be with her immediately,' Hannah said. 'And Mrs Bell?'

'Yes, madam?'

'Please instruct Susan to bring my daughter to us. She is more in need of a wardrobe than I am.'

'Very well, madam,' the housekeeper said as she turned and exited the room.

★ ★ ★

Slowly the weeks passed. As Hannah sat at Edward's bedside, stitching a petticoat for her daughter while he dozed, her mind would stray inexorably to the little market town in spreading countryside where she had left her heart.

Now that she was estranged from the mill she could accept that she had fallen in love with Cameron Blake. It had been a gradual process, mutual regard blossoming into friendship and then something deeper and more wonderful.

She had only to recall his fiery crop of hair, his big, surprisingly gentle hands and twinkling deep-blue gaze and her heart would suffer a pang.

She wondered whether Thomas had persuaded his father to allow him to follow a life at sea and if young Will had kept to his path as a horse-breaker.

There was Madge — dear, kindly Madge. How Hannah missed her; their chats over a pot of tea, kittens on the hearth and Vinnie gurgling on the mat at their feet. Strangely, the dreams that had been so illuminating had ceased. Not once since she had returned to Croft House had the past reached out to her.

'You are reflective, my dear,' Edward said one dismal day in November. A bright fire burned in the grate and the leaping flames threw shadows on the linen-fold panelling and rich velour hangings that adorned the room.

'A little,' Hannah admitted.

'Are you unhappy? Would you rather have stayed away from here and followed your own vision?'

'Edward, I came back. I had to make amends. It was my place at your side.'

'Not for much longer, I warrant.' Edward's mouth worked slowly as he tried to form the right words. 'Hannah, I am plainly not long for this life. You are young and lovely to look upon and could make some fellow extremely happy. Promise me that when I am gone, you will marry again. And this time to a younger man, someone who will be good to you — and to our daughter.'

Hannah was silent. There was only one she wanted, and he could never be hers. Chances were he was wed by now and the millhouse had a new mistress.

She thought of the Blakes — handsome Thomas, reprobate Will, Miller Blake himself, his twinkling smile and gravelly voice. Reflecting on the daintily-attired Lizzie Marsh faced with a daily battle of flour-encrusted clothing and the tramp of muddy boots, quite without rancour a smile touched Hannah's lips.

'Ah, you are brighter already. Was there someone you met during your sojourn in the south of the county? Some admirer, perhaps?' he asked.

Hannah shook her head sadly. 'Edward, please, let us not speak of this. You are a little stronger today. The doctor commented on it when he called. His treatments must be doing you some good.'

''Tis the sight of you that does me

the most good, my dear.'

'Thank you, Edward. Is there anything you require? Perhaps I might read to you for a while. Shall it be Mr Dickens?'

'Not just yet. Hannah, there is one thing. There are certain issues I need to square at the boatyard.'

'But Doctor Gilchrist said — '

'I know what he said, confound it! Point is I've left one or two things in the air and they've got to be settled. Everything else is sorted. My man of law has the will drawn up and witnessed. The bulk of the estate goes to you.'

'Edward, I do not expect — '

'Wife, let me finish. In the event of your remarriage, you will receive a generous allowance and the rest will go as Delyth's portion. There are bequests to my other daughters, naturally, and others to friends and associates. There should be no quibbles on that score. It is just these one or two small matters at the boatyard that need addressing.'

'You wish me to summon the manager? Greasby?' Hannah suppressed a sudden shudder. Much time had passed and yet the memory of the boatyard manager's unwelcome advances still had the power to bring a wave of chill to her flesh.

'Greasby?' Edward repeated. 'Has no one told you? Harry Greasby's gone. I caught the fellow conducting a neat little sideline of his own — and on my time and expense, I might add. I sent him packing. Odd thing, there always was something about him I didn't trust, just couldn't put my finger on it. Amazing tool, instinct, don't you think?'

'Yes,' Hannah agreed, relieved beyond measure that never again would she see the overseer's leering grin and hungry gaze.

'The new man goes by the name of Cartwright. Nathaniel Cartwright. He came to me from at a yard at Moreton, a smaller concern than Pennington's but thriving all the same. He's a good fellow, totally trustworthy and isn't afraid of a bit of hard work either. And he's not unschooled in social graces.' Edward paused, gnawing thoughtfully on his bottom lip. 'Cartwright's what you'd call a man of the times. Makes me regret I'll not be around long enough to see how things progress with him. Has my daughter never mentioned how cleverly he lightens the mood at the dinner table?'

'Delyth? Why, no. This is the first I have heard.'

'That does surprise me. Still, never mind. Rest assured that you can rely on Cartwright's integrity if need be. Best you meet him, Hannah. You will send word that I wish to see him right away, will you?'

'Very well,' she agreed. 'Make sure you do not tire yourself, that is all, Edward.'

'Tire myself? Lying here in this confounded bed day in, day out, supping potions and being fed pobs like a babe? Wife, how could I do that?'

It was bravado speaking. Ten days later, all loose ends satisfactorily tied, Edward Pennington breathed his last.

It was a peaceful end with his daughters gathered around him. Edward Pennington had been a well-respected figure and Hannah, swept along on the grim tide of burial arrangements and other necessities, scarcely had the time to give any thought to anything but the immediate requirements.

It was not until afterwards, the last mourner gone and the house quiet and black-draped, that the full force of what had happened and its implications was brought home to her. She was a young widow with a small child, more than adequately catered for, with her life stretching before her — empty and without any purpose. For those first dark weeks of mourning, that was how it remained.

'That is the third sigh in as many minutes,' Delyth said one afternoon. February sleet slithered down the window pane. She had forsaken her usual seat in the window embrasure for the comfort of the fireside. 'Hannah, are you quite well?'

'Oh, yes, thank you. I was just thinking.'

'About Papa? You mustn't fret, you know. You made him happy, those last weeks.'

'And before that? Delyth, I was the object of a great deal of worry and humiliation. I never gave a thought as to how it might be for your father when I ran away.'

'You were driven to it. Oh, I know one shouldn't speak ill of the dead. I loved Papa as was my duty as a daughter, but I also knew him. He was not the easiest of persons. Hannah, you must not reproach yourself. You more than made up for what happened by returning and devoting yourself to nursing Papa during his final days. If you continue in this way, you could make yourself ill. You've a child to think of, remember. What would Vinnie do if you were taken badly?'

'I won't be. I am never ill. I am simply trying to come to terms with everything.'

Hannah knew that Delyth's words were right but, reason as she might, the fog of guilt and remorse that clouded her days and tortured her nights was not a simple matter to shrug off. She told herself she had done her best for Edward. Nursed him tirelessly, read to him until her eyes ached and her voice was no more than a croak, assisted him with the various small worries connected with the business, soothed him when the solace of sleep would not come. It had been all she could think of to make amends and yet it had never seemed enough, and it still did not.

'Have you thought what you will do now?' Delyth said, putting aside her embroidery.

'Do?' Hannah turned her weary eyes on her stepdaughter.

'Yes. Oh, granted you have Vinnie to bring up and you are mistress of the house. Then again, you are not one to fill your days with tea-parties and callers.'

'No,' Hannah said darkly. 'It is probably no bad thing. I suspect that once the period of mourning is past I shall find myself remarkably lacking on that score. Up to now people have accepted me, largely because your father was still there to act as a buffer. I'd be a fool to expect it to continue. If there is one thing I have learned, it is that it does not do to marry out of one's class. To Edward's associates I am the conniving miss he dragged out of the gutter and I always will be.'

'Oh, fie! You were hardly that, Hannah. What you forget is that Papa was the son of an ordinary fisher family himself. It was his knowledge and expertise that bought him his passage into society.'

'People forget when it suits.' Hannah sighed. 'What you say is true. I shall have to think about an occupation. As far as I can see, I have two choices. To stay put and run Croft House, or to pass that responsibility to you and look for a project of my own.'

'You'd do that, Hannah?' It was a rhetorical question and Delyth continued quickly, 'Yes, I believe you would. Have you any ideas on the matter?'

It came to Hannah all at once and she sat upright, her face brightening for the first time in as many weeks.

'Yes, I have. I've always had a fancy to have a business of my own. It has been nothing more than a dream . . . until now.'

Delyth gazed at her. 'A shop, you mean? Like Verity Talbot's haberdashery on the Parade? Papa admired her nerve, you know. People said she would never make a success of it but she has, many times over.'

'You think it a good move?'

'Well, you could do worse. We shall have to consult the Parkgate Agents as to what premises are available.'

Hannah's mind ran ahead. No, not Parkgate. She would only be frowned upon or even avoided. And Chester was too big and crowded; she never had felt at home in the city. Where else could she go? As always, her mind slowly drifted back to the quaint market town that her mother had remembered with such clarity and fondness.

'Delyth, do you recall the lack of lodgings there was at Malpas for ladies travelling alone?'

'Yes, I remember it well. I thought it strange for so busy a township to lack such a facility.' She paused, eyes widening. 'Hannah, you are thinking to open a boarding house for gentlewomen there?'

'It is an idea.'

The more Hannah reflected on the notion, the better it appealed. She would be doing the community a service and this, she felt, might assuage the damaging guilt she was experiencing. Added to which, it would be fulfilling.

Edward, as he had impressed upon her, had left her in sole command of his assets until such time as she remarried, when she would receive a portion as a yearly allowance and the house and business would go to his youngest. As things stood, Hannah had the funds to carry out her scheme. She had the enthusiasm and the capacity for work.

She would be in the bitter-sweet vicinity of Cameron Blake, be able to watch his children grow up, whispered a small inner voice that would not be ignored.

'What fun!' Delyth sent her a smile, her plain face gaining a sudden charm. 'Indeed, I have half a mind to join you.'

'Oh, I do not think you would. It would mean leaving your home and all that you hold dear. And what of Mr Cartwright? Am I right in saying that you and he seem to get on remarkably well together?' she asked.

Delyth blushed. 'You have noticed.'

'I would have been blind not to. I wonder, had your father something other than the boatyard in mind when he took on Nathaniel Cartwright as his manager?'

'What makes you say that?'

'He made a point of impressing upon me what an excellent character Mr Cartwright has. He said it more than once. He obviously knew he was leaving the business in capable hands, but there was more to it than that. Mr Cartwright had become a regular guest at the dinner table, I believe.'

'Yes. That is how we came to know each other. Hannah, I confess I do like Nathaniel. I like him a lot and I suspect he feels the same way about me. Of course, being in mourning . . . '

Hannah reached out and touched the younger woman's arm affectionately. 'Dearest Delyth. If anything comes of it and I've an idea it will, rest assured that you have my absolute blessing.'

'You would not mind? According to the terms of Papa's will, it would mean our living here, at Croft House.'

'What of it? The house is large enough to accommodate more than one family. Always supposing I am still here.'

'You will go with your scheme?'

'I shall certainly make inquiries once the period of mourning is over. If I do go ahead, Susan must come with me — she has a smart head on her shoulders.' Already Hannah's mind was grappling with figures and furnishing and the possibilities of staffing. 'I confess I feel better already. And see, I do believe the sun is trying to get through. It must be an omen.'

Before she had the chance to put anything into practice, before even she was able to draw breath, Hannah had a visitor.

15

'There is a gentleman to see you, madam. I've shown him into the library,' Mrs Bell announced.

The dissention in the housekeeper's voice was only thinly disguised and Hannah's curiosity as to who the caller could be was overlaid by the usual sense of irritation laced with amusement. Really, there was no accounting for Mrs Bell!

'Thank you, Mrs Bell. Could you take Vinnie to the nursery for me? Off you go, Vinnie. Tell Susan we had a nice walk and fed the ducks, won't you?'

The child nodded, smiling. Hannah thought how pretty she looked in her white muslin frills and pink sash, her dark hair coaxed into ringlets.

'Very well, madam. Come along, Miss Vinnie. Take Mrs Bell's hand. We don't want to tumble on the stairs, do we?'

Even Mrs Bell was not immune to Vinnie's charms and Hannah saw a smile touch the woman's lips as she took command of the child. As they proceeded up the stairs Hannah checked her appearance in the looking glass. The violet of semi-mourning was not unbecoming, though her cheeks were pale despite the walk in the blustery March air. She pinched some colour into them, tucking an errant curl away beneath her widow's cap. Satisfied that she presented an image as became her position, she continued to the library.

In the doorway, Hannah froze. The burly figure in country fustian and gaiters, boots buffed to a fine shine and a tangle of burnished-auburn hair for once tamed to smoothness, not a speck of flour dust to be seen on his person, was entirely unexpected. He was standing with his back to her, studying the portrait of Edward's first wife that hung above the mantelpiece, and did not at first notice that he was not alone.

'Cameron!'

He turned and the smile that lit his bearded face caused Hannah's heart to beat all the faster.

'Hannah. Or should I say Mrs Pennington.'

'I'm Hannah to you, always will be. Oh, Cameron!' She sped across the room and stood before him, looking up into his face as if she could never get enough of the sight of him. 'What a lovely surprise. How good it is to see you.'

'I'm sorry it wasn't sooner. We've only now heard the sad news of your loss. Hannah, please accept our deepest sympathy at this difficult time.'

The rumbling country voice was music to her ears. 'Thank you. Edward suffered. I think in the end it was a release.'

'And yourself? These past months must have been hard.'

'I am well, thank you.'

'What of the little maid? Growing apace, I expect?' 'Yes, she is.' Hannah smiled. 'You must see Vinnie before you go.'

'I should like that. I've booked a room at the inn for tonight. My horse is stabled there.'

'You've ridden here?' she asked with some surprise, Cameron's aversion to the saddle being legendary.

'There are matters I had to speak to you about. Will had a horse he's let me use.'

'I see,' Hannah said, utterly perplexed. He sounded serious and, condolences apart, she wondered what it was that was so urgent as to instigate a long and uncomfortable journey to see her. 'Tell me, how are they all?'

'All fine and dandy. There have been changes. Thomas applied for his ticket. He sailed last month for the Americas — and with Father's blessing I might add.'

'Thomas has gone to sea?' Hannah said with surprise, adding quietly, 'May

God watch over him.'

'Amen to that. We're not seafaring folk as you know, bar Great-Uncle Bertie and he was one on his own. The closest the rest of us get to water is a swim in the millstream to cool off on a hot summer's day!'

They both laughed and the atmosphere lightened a little.

'What about Sally? What does she say to it all?'

'She wept at first but I think she's resigned. Better a husband that's absent half the year than one who grows bitter in an occupation he doesn't care for. They're planning to wed when his ship comes home.'

'Oh, that is wonderful news. And young Will? Still the same rapscallion, is he?'

'He'll always be a law unto himself! He's knuckled down to work now Thomas is no longer here, but every spare minute is spent with his horses. He's building up quite a reputation for himself. The Marquis of Cholmondeley has sent him a couple of hunters to be broken.'

'Oh my! What did Will say to that?'

'Couldn't keep the smile from his face! They're sending him another once this current job's done; a handy mare the Marquis wants schooling up for his lady.'

'That will involve getting the animal used to a sidesaddle, I would say. Will Lizzie help there?'

'Ah, Lizzie!'

Cameron's face changed and Hannah felt a quiver of alarm. Putting off what she was convinced could be difficult news for her guest to impart she took refuge behind her duties as a hostess. 'Oh, look at me! You have ridden all this way and I keep you talking. You must be in dire need of refreshment. Let me ring for tea.'

Sending her a long, unfathomable look, Cameron went to sit in a high-backed chair by the fireside. Hannah pulled the bell and took the seat opposite and they made small talk until Susan came in with the tea-tray. After the maid had retreated, Hannah poured the tea and waited while her guest fell hungrily upon the daintily-prepared sandwiches of smoked salmon and muffins kept warm under a silver lid.

Having eaten his fill, Cameron put aside his napkin, sat back in his chair and looked at her levelly. 'Hannah, I have to tell you this. It's all over between Lizzie and me. I'd known for some while she wasn't the right one for me and I think, in her heart, she knew it too.'

'You have broken off the betrothal? Oh, Cameron!'

'It isn't as bad as it appears. In fact Lizzie has come off rather well over it. She's found another suitor, one who is able to give her the sort of life she craves. I could never have done that. Could you in all honesty have seen Lizzie as mistress of the millhouse? I couldn't, and the longer things went on the more I came to realise it. She'd been brought up to be looked after, not to be at the beck and call of a bunch of men. Once the first gloss had worn off, she'd have been unhappy.'

Hannah took a moment or two to digest this revelation. 'I do understand your reasoning. Do I know the future husband?'

'Yes, you do. It's Weston Prosser, the mine owner.'

'Prosser? Glory be!'

'Seems he'd had his eye on Lizzie for a while. They both attend St Oswald's. He raised his cap to her one Sunday as she left the church and things went from there.'

'Well!' Hannah was lost for words.

'I reckon they stand every chance of making the ideal couple. Lizzie's got some learning about her and Prosser will favour that. Felicia Black has gone, by the way.'

'Gone?'

'Perhaps I'd best start at the beginning. What I have to say concerns you.' He paused, his eyes looking very blue in his outdoor face. 'It all came about the week after Christmas. I'd called to see Madge Nightingale and stayed on to chop her some firewood.'

'Madge! I haven't asked after her! How remiss of me. How is she?' she enquired.

'Spry as ever. She sends you and Vinnie her love. Where was I? Oh yes. I was leaving Brook Cottage when who should come along the road in the gig but Prosser. He drew up and offered a lift. It was a raw sort of day and I took him up on it. He said he'd been meaning to come and see me about an issue that had been on his mind for some while. Turned out he'd been working late one night and needed some information that was in Miss Black's desk. He'd got a spare key and went to get what was wanted. When he tried to close the drawer again it wouldn't shut properly. On investigation he found a purse of coins wedged right at the back.'

'Was it . . . the money I was accused of taking?'

'Seems so. He counted it out and the amount tallied exactly with the missing sum. He went straight to Miss Black's door and confronted her and it all came out. She said how jealous she'd been of you, how she'd wanted to bring you down.'

'And succeeded,' Hannah said quietly.

'She hadn't quite the gall to take the money herself so she'd stuffed it out of sight in her desk. It was the end of her position at the mine. Prosser sends his deepest apologies and hopes you will find it in your heart to forgive him.'

'You told him about my situation; who I really was?'

'He already knew. Apparently he'd been curious about you and made some enquiries of his own. I suspect he'd had some notion of making you his bride. Discovering you were already wed must have come as a shock.'

Hannah recalled her last day at the Dirtwich mine, her employer being called out on some mission and coming back in a rage, the horse lathered as if it had been ridden hard. Was this what he had been about? It would explain a great deal.

She said, 'I admit to being wrong in many ways, but I would never have stolen from him — or anyone.'

'I think he knew that. No man likes to be thwarted. Your not being free to marry would have coloured his judgment. Incidentally, Prosser said to impress upon you that your secret was safe with him. Oddly enough, I trust him.'

Cameron smiled at her encouragingly before going on. 'Hannah, there's more.'

It turned out that Madge Nightingale had remembered Hannah having once dropped her guard and mentioning how the snowy weather they had had the previous winter had not been so on the coast.

'It was obvious you'd had first-hand experience of it, though she was too tactful to say. She'd also noticed a piece of jewellery you took pains to conceal about your person.'

Hannah's hand went to the silver locket she now wore for all to see. 'It was my mother's. She told me it had belonged to the aunt who had brought her up.'

'That would have been Hannah Mary Carraway. She visited Brook Cottage with her niece, a child by the name of Alice.'

'Alice was my mother. Hannah Mary was my great-aunt. When I was born Mother gave me her name, only I'm Hannah Alice Rose after Mother, and Father's mother.'

'Madge couldn't remember the name of the man Alice eventually married but she thought he was a sea-going fellow. Other things fell into place. She said how Vinnie bore a resemblance to the child Alice. She couldn't credit how it had never occurred to her before. Apparently Alice was fond of going into town. From a very early age it was where she liked most to be. Madge thought she hankered after the hustle and bustle. Agden must have been pretty quiet for a girl in those days.'

'I had always believed my mother was a Malpas person but I was wrong. She originated from a village called Wrenbury.'

'On the road to Nantwich? I know it well. We sometimes deal with a miller near there, at Swanley. What a small world it is.'

'I remember Madge once saying that, but I don't know so much. It can seem very large and inhospitable at times.'

Cameron's eyes softened. 'Hannah, lass. You must have felt very much alone.'

'I had Vinnie, and there was Madge. And then I came to the mill and it was almost like being part of the family.' Something in Cameron's expression caused her to bite her lip. She went on hastily, 'Mother was only a babe when she left Wrenbury and would not have had any memory of it. I expect Hannah Mary never spoke of it, given the reason why they moved away. Did Madge tell you?'

'Your mama being motherless and deserted by her papa? Yes, she did. What a shocking business. Was your mama happy in her own marriage?'

'Oh, yes! She liked Parkgate but she always cherished a feeling for Malpas. It's where she met my father. The man who dealt with the deliveries for the fishmonger businesses was indisposed and Father stood in for him. He came to Mother's rescue when her bonnet fell off and nearly got trampled in the traffic. They used to laugh about it.' Her face grew sombre.

'Father was a fisherman by trade. One day his boat was heading the fleet when a storm blew up. A man went overboard and Father dived to the rescue. Both were lost.'

'Dear God! Were you very young at the time?'

'I was in my tenth year, plenty old enough to remember what a fine man he was. After he died, Mother worked her fingers to the bone to keep us. I would go gleaning with her on the fields and to work with the fisher-wives on the shore. When I grew up I didn't want that. Mother had taught me well and when she passed on, I applied for work as a governess. That is how I came to meet Edward. His eldest daughter had two children by then and Edward advertised for a governess for them. The daughter had a fine house at Meols. I really thought I had come up in the world when I went there. Edward would visit.'

'And fell in love with you. Who could blame him?'

'We were fish and fowl. Once I saw where things were heading, I should have looked for a position elsewhere. I thought of it but I could not bring myself to go ahead. I was so afraid of ending up scratching a living like Mother had to . . . and I confess I was flattered by the attention Edward gave me.'

'It isn't easy for womenfolk. You did

what you felt right at the time. Edward Pennington must have thought a lot of you.'

'Well, he took me back, did he not? Few men would have done that.'

'His gain was our loss. We have missed you, Hannah. I missed you more than I can say.'

Silence fell. Their eyes met. Hannah was first to look away.

'It has been a problem knowing what to do now that I am widowed,' she said with a change of tack. 'There is nothing here for Vinnie and me. I was discussing it with Delyth and I thought I would return to Malpas and start a boarding house there for lone lady travellers.'

He looked startled. 'A boarding house? Is this what you really want, Hannah?'

'There is demand. I would be doing a public service. I have to do something with my life,' she said vehemently.

'Oh, Hannah.'

Again their eyes met. Again the silence. The ormolu clock on the mantelpiece chimed the hour. The quiet dragged on, until Cameron rose abruptly and came across to her. Taking her hands, he eased her to her feet.

'Hannah, if this is what you wish then I'll not argue the point, though I have to say this. I love you. I think I've loved you ever since the day we met. There I was, mazed and winnocky after a fall from the horse and this vision appeared. Glory be, I thought I'd died and gone to heaven!'

'I must have looked a tearful angel,' Hannah said ruefully. 'I was seeking work and could not find any.'

'Do you believe in a great pattern of things? Call me fanciful if you like, but I do.'

'A pattern? I do not know.' She thought of the dreams, the discovery of the journal in the millhouse attic, even the way her steps had taken her to Madge Nightingale's door when she was at her lowest ebb. 'Maybe.'

Cameron placed his gentle, work-roughened hands on her shoulders. He was so close she could smell the cloth of his topcoat and the warm, masculine tang of horse and harness leather that hung about him. He personified all that was good and kind and strong.

'Hannah, I am a free man now. I came here with some notion of asking you to be my wife. I'd be a loving and faithful husband to you and a good father to your child. You have my word on that. I allow 'tis early days yet for you. Perhaps, when you've had time to get over your bereavement you would consider my — '

He said no more, for Hannah stood on tiptoe and silenced him with a kiss full on the lips. After a brief, startled hesitation his face lit up and his arms enclosed her in a hug that wonderfully, gloriously, all but took her breath away.

Next moment he was twirling her round, dancing with her amongst the clutter of small spindly tables and fragile knick-knacks, astonishingly light on his feet for so huge a man, dancing until she pleaded for mercy.

'Of course I'll marry you, you great ox!' she said, breathlessly, when he came to a stop. 'It's all I've ever dreamed of. Oh, Cameron. I love you too. I always have. I fought it. I tried and tried not to let it show. I even tried to be harsh with you and oh, it was hard.'

'You're sure? You won't mind leaving all this?'

'Of course not. We shall be together for the rest of our lives. What more could I want? Just think. I shall be able to tell Vinnie she is coming back to Malpas.'

'Coming home,' Cameron said and, taking her once more into his arms, he sealed the pledge with a tender kiss.

We do hope that you have enjoyed reading this large print book.

Did you know that all of our titles are available for purchase?

We publish a wide range of high quality large print books including:
Romances, Mysteries, Classics
General Fiction
Non Fiction and Westerns

Special interest titles available in large print are:
The Little Oxford Dictionary
Music Book, Song Book
Hymn Book, Service Book

Also available from us courtesy of Oxford University Press:
Young Readers' Dictionary
(large print edition)
Young Readers' Thesaurus
(large print edition)

For further information or a free brochure, please contact us at:
Ulverscroft Large Print Books Ltd.,
The Green, Bradgate Road, Anstey,
Leicester, LE7 7FU, England.
Tel: (00 44) 0116 236 4325
Fax: (00 44) 0116 234 0205

SOMETHING'S BREWING

Wendy Kremer

When Kate's job as a superstore manager comes to an abrupt end, she takes a risk and signs the lease to a seafront café. After hiring a teenage girl to work weekends, Kate is shocked to learn that her uncle is Ryan Scott, her former boss. He's tall, dark, attractive — and in Kate's opinion, arrogant. As she opens for business, she begins to see a different side to him. But with a café to run, Kate doesn't have time to think about Ryan, or any other man . . .

MEETING MOLLY

Chrissie Loveday

With £4.07 in her bank account, the rent due, and her party-planning business foundering, Sarah-Louise is forced to look for a job. Spotting one in the paper, she makes the call and soon meets Olly, who is looking after his sister's dog Molly for six months and needs someone to walk her. Sarah-Louise takes a fancy to him — but after dealing with an AWOL Molly, a jealous flatmate and a worrying attack on Olly, could the two of them possibly have a future together?

NEVER LET YOU GO

Sarah Purdue

When Sofia Garcia's fiancé Jack says he needs space and then drops off the radar, she takes up her uncle's offer of a job as a tour guide in Spain, determined to move on with her life. But when she recognises a name on her latest guest list, she can't believe it's *her* Jack, who she hasn't heard from in eight months — he's come to Spain to try to win her back. Can Sofia find a way to trust him again, and is she prepared to risk her heart once more?

THE RANSOM

Irena Nieslony

Eve Masters's life is thrown into chaos when her beloved David is kidnapped on their home island of Crete. Determined to track down those involved, Eve finds herself at odds with the police and suspecting her own friends. Then David escapes; but, ill and unable to remember who his kidnappers were, he is rushed to hospital — where someone tries to silence him for good. Can Eve get to the bottom of the mystery before the kidnappers turn their sights on her?

ENCHANTED NURSE

Phyllis Mallet

English nurse Karyn Gregory believes her new post on the Greek island of Sporveza will be a dream come true. But it's not all smooth sailing as she meets her challenging charge, Nerissa, a young woman haunted by the accident that caused the deaths of her parents. Unable to walk, she blames herself for the tragedy, hiding herself away in the gloomy attic of the cliffside house. And how is Nerissa's handsome brother, Paul, involved with the mysterious darker side of the island — one that is stained with blood?